a PLace caLLeD DeLIrIUM

avaaNTIKa KaKKar

A PLACE CALLED DELIRIUM Copyright ©2016

Line By Lion Publications
318 Louis Coleman Jr. Drive
Louisville, KY 40212
www.linebylion.com

ISBN: 978-1940938-76-9

They flash upon that inward eye
Which is the bliss of solitude...
- William Wordsworth, *The Daffodils*

Man is essentially a dreamer, wakened sometimes for a moment by some peculiarly obtrusive element in the outer world, but lapsing again quickly into the happy world of somnolence and imagination.

- Bertrand Russell, *Sceptical Essays*

PROLOGUE

Indian Naval Hospital Ship Asvini, Colaba, Mumbai, 26/11/2008, 10:30 P.M.

Debbie had the shrillest voice. It was worse over the phone. It did not help when AJ asked her to calm down - her voice only went up a few decibels.

The news had sunk in. Debbie was sobbing into her phone. It would be useless to ask her to stop.

"Debbie, don't cry, please. It will be alright."

"How do you know? What about the baby?"

"The baby will be fine. Some things don't happen to us. Meera's a fighter, you know that."

AJ was helpless. They were all helpless tonight. You had to stay in and hope that someone would take care of the terrorists, and that it would all end soon.

"AJ, this *has* happened to us. Her phone is soaked in blood, AJ and it was so weird. Her face, the look in her eyes, and she was smiling at me, past the smears of blood and sweat and tears and muck and she was singing, AJ. Her face keeps flashing in front of my eyes."

"Singing?"

"Something about a dream. I have a dream or something? That was all I could make out. She was trying to sing it."

"I have a dream? A fantasy? ABBA, don't you remember? *If you see the won-der…of the fairy tales…you can take the fu-ture, even if you fail…*and so on."

"She didn't sound like that at all. It was quite garbled. What was she doing at the Taj Palace Hotel, of all places, tonight? How will it end? Will she die, AJ?"

"Of course she won't, Deb. How strange that you should ask me that. I asked her the same thing when we spoke over the phone last night. I think it may have even been around the same time. I asked her if he would die in the end."

"Who? Who would die in the end?"

"Dennis Quaid."

"*Who?*"

"I will tell you, Deb. About Dennis Quaid and this movie called, *Savior*. But now, before the lines are jammed, I am going to call her family and let them know. Okay?"

CHAPTER 1

NIGHT
The *Kuber*, somewhere off the coast of Mumbai, 25/11/2008, 10:30 P.M.

Aboard the *Kuber*, a group of young Pakistani men take turns at manning the watchtower and guarding the hostage captain, Amar Sinh. They have orders to kill him when they are done with him.

The young Pakistanis are nervous but trained to remain calm. This is, after all, the path to heaven.

The home port of the *Kuber* is Porbandar, Gujarat. But the vessel is registered in Mumbai and Gujarat. Nothing should go wrong. They had come so far.

These men will not hurt Amar Sinh as long as he mans the vessel and gets them to Mumbai. They will then brutally kill him. They are heavily armed and watch him closely. They will kill him like they killed the rest of his crew. He prays that it is not too painful. Then he tries not to think about it. Maybe they will let him go. Maybe he will escape, get to the police and warn them about these Pakistanis, their weapons and supplies. He will see his family again. His children. He will return home, maybe. Maybe, the coastguard will intercept this vessel and foil their plans. This is why Amar sails on, guiding the *Kuber* to the shores of Mumbai.

Sneh Sadan, Colaba, Mumbai, 25/11/2008, 10:30 P.M.

"Will he die in the end?"

"You know what AJ, we are wasting time."

"What do you mean?"

"This movie will stretch over two hours, it may or may not be good, and we are what we like to call, 'chilling'. But this is two hours of our lives and Dennis Quaid may, as you suggest, die in the end. Why are we watching this? Let's just read a spoiler on the internet and get on with it. There is so much that can be achieved in two hours."

"Get on with what, Meera? What do you want to achieve in the next two hours? Do you know what day of the week it is?"

"It's Tuesday, the 25th of November 2008, you idiot. And I don't know what I want to achieve in the next two hours. But we are running out of time. Before we know it, we will be old. And dying. And we will not remember

Savior or these two hours and how we did not use them."

"Can we just please continue with the movie? Please?"

"You really want to do this?"

"Yes. Come on. Will he die in the end?"

"Hmmm. You are asking too soon because the movie's just starting. A lot has happened though, we are not even twenty minutes into the film and they blew Dennis Quaid's wife and kid up, then he killed those people in the mosque as revenge, and now he and his friend are in Bosnia in 1993, escaped criminals, reduced to mercenaries fighting other people's wars. You know, AJ, I know this guy who is playing Quaid's friend. Can't remember his name. He was the guy in *The Glass House*. He played Terry Glass…he was the villain."

"Stellan S-K-A-R-S-G-A-R-D. How do you pronounce that? With the 'a' spelt with that circle on top like, 'å'. I don't know how to pronounce it."

"Of course! Stellan Skarsgård. Let's call him 'Stellan'. Did you like *The Glass House*? I did."

"Haven't watched it. I just Googled it."

"Such a cheat you are! Quaid's wife was really overacting, you know? Bit part. Emoted with her eyes before the director asked her to play dead."

"They told her in acting class that actors emote with their eyes."

"That's the only thing she remembered. She tried too hard. She became an emoticon with her eyes and jammed the rest of her muscles."
"An emoticon? Ha ha."

"I don't like kids dying, AJ."

"It's a movie."

"But they do die in real life. And no one knows their unfinished stories. It's unnatural."

"Now I know. Quaid will die in the end. You just finished the movie for me. Thanks."

"Why?"

"His wife and kid are dead. They were killed in front of him. He is a murderer on the run who works as a mercenary. What does he live for?"

"Then he should just kill himself, AJ."

"That would make it a very short movie."

"I like short stories."

"No you don't. *Wuthering Heights* and *Pride & Prejudice* are not short stories."

"You should really read *Emma*, AJ."

"*Emma's* not a short story, either."

"Up yours. So Quaid's on the Bosnian side. Against the Muslims. Stellan Skarsgård is smoking pot...I think. He has that look, you know? He wants to give this up, thinks they haven't been doing the right thing. I'll say! Quaid says they haven't done anything wrong and that he will miss him. That's it. Poor Stellan Skarsgård. He was only being a friend and got dragged into this. Quaid is going with some local guy for a hostage exchange. You aren't bored, AJ?"

"I like it when you tell stories. What will you do tomorrow when Hubby flies off to Singapore?"

"I don't know. I am going to think my thoughts through. Happy to be alone and all that. I may take the day off. Now focus, Quaid has found a baby in the cupboard of a house that he and this local-guy or soldier barged into. He surreptitiously puts on a pacifier. Why? Will Local Soldier kill it? Local Soldier enters room. Misbehaves with corpses. Oh no. He's going to kill the old woman who lies sobbing on the bed. Pulling out a dagger behind his back. Why doesn't Quaid do something?

Jesus! Come on! He cut off her finger…for a ring. She's screaming. Local Soldier wears the bloodied ring while the old woman howls in the background. That was creepy."

"Just a movie, Mee. Listen, should you be watching this stuff?"

"No. But I'm fine. Was it Bosnian Muslims or Serbian Muslims? And who out there had a problem with who? Who started it? For a lawyer, my idea of political history is mind numbingly limited. Wasn't there a war tribunal and all set up? Did we not moot about all of this in the International Law class?"

"Yah. I remember how the news used to be full of it. I've forgotten the details. But then, I'm not a lawyer. Listen, don't watch this flick. Why did you even pick this movie? Who raises his hand screaming, 'Dennis Quaid!' when asked to list the actors one likes to watch? What were you thinking?"
"I know. I know. It isn't physically possible to kick yourself, is it? Hey, AJ? They killed Stellan Skarsgård off, man. That's why he's not with Quaid to pick up the hostage and that's why Quaid is stuck with the Native Asshole."

"Great. Quaid's *really* got nothing now. He needed Stellan. *I* needed Stellan. Give the man some hope! No family. No friends. He's going to die now. I know. Good night."

"This has to be one of the worst films I ever picked. *Savior*? Seriously."

"Stop watching it, Mee."

"AJ, do you want to hang up? You can't seriously listen to the whole movie just to keep me company!"

"Tell you what. I am going to call you in five. Not because I don't want to do this but because first, I need a drink like now, before we grow old. And second, I need the popcorn to do this right. I will call you, okay?"

"Alright. But I won't hold it against you if you don't call back. Bye."

*   *   *

– right. One of the hostages who they are picking up in the exchange is a woman. She's pregnant. Local Guy knows her. They were neighbors. He's gonna take her home in their car.

I am alone. Shall I do it?

Will have to draw the curtains. Is anyone at that window? They are the only ones who can see what's going on in here.

No. No one's at the window. But what's to stop them from wandering to their window? To see you, touching it…there.

Screw it. Who wants to get up? Damn the curtains. Not in the mood. I have a headache. Not tonight. Ha ha. I'm so funny.

The movie does not inspire it. Should have brought the Titanic. Kate and DiCaprio do it for me, especially when they look at each other.

Excuse me? She was taken hostage. You, idiot?

That's right, Quaid. Tell Local Guy. She was raped. She lives just like you still live after seeing your wife and kid dead and after killing all those people in that mosque. Yes. We all live, don't we? Local Guy's ranting. She has betrayed her family's honor. Honor? What do you know about it, you…? You wore the ring, still bloodied. Cut off that old woman's finger…

Tunnel.

I love tunnels. You stare out of the train thinking you can see the darkness…listening to the rhythm of the train…straining, peering into the black dark darkness and think you see the rough edges of blasted rock…till you realize that you cannot. Then, suddenly, the light. And it doesn't matter anymore because you return to staring at the well-lit countryside thanks to those bright lamps, the sun and the moon, and sometimes, when they work at it, the stars.

What the …!

Local Guy kicks the daylight out of the-hostage-who-got-pregnant-in-captivity. She's going to die, idiot. Which side are you on?

Gunshot.

Thanks, Dennis! That was necessary. Oh! He is sweet. He is helping with the childbirth…all that kicking induced labour…he is sweet. I hope he lives. –

*   *   *

"Hi! So you did call back, AJ."

"Why not? So, have you got to the part where she starts feeding the baby?"

"How do you know? Have you watched this before?"

"No. I am reading the spoilers online."

"AJ, you are an ass. Quaid should get the Oscar. He helped deliver the baby. They are huge when they're born. Huge. She tried killing herself. Quaid stops her. He took her home…"

It is good to speak with AJ after this long. He had called just about the time that the movie was starting. They hadn't bothered with picking up the threads – it was as if they'd only spoken yesterday.

The doorbell does not startle her. She had been waiting for it to ring.

"Hey! He's home!"

"Alright then! This is where I sign off! You bore him with the movie now, girl. And tell him I said, 'Hullo'!"

"You wasted time. Precious time. I told you we were wasting time."

"But I am going to use the time now, just got an alert that the Federal Reserve has announced a US$ 800 billion stimulus package."

"Bye, you. It was boring, wasn't it?"

"Only a little. Tell me if he dies in the end, though."

"Read the spoilers for that! After you have the update on the package they announced."

*   *   *

"What are you watching?" he asks loosening his tie, noticing her dazed look and the glowing television in the living room.

Savior.

He's been working late. In quiet exchange for her pleasant tolerance he joins her on the sofa.

He is not really interested in the movie. He smells nice. His quick nighttime wash has removed neither the residue of the musky perfume nor the scent of a long day at work. She looks at him, his eyes focused intently on Dennis Quaid, who in this frame holds the baby.

He turns to her, "What's happening, Meera?"

"You look sexy!"

He smiles, "You look cute. That is his baby?"

"If you change that to 'you look beautiful', I will tell you where we are at with the movie."

He says it.

Happily, she summarises the movie for him. "It is about the Bosnian-Serb conflict. Quaid's rescued a woman who was raped in captivity and saves her from one crazy soldier. Mad fellow. If he was such a hero, why the hell did he not kill her captors? Anyway, after all that trouble, her family does not accept her...the mother does but that doesn't matter because her dad doesn't. So Quaid's taking her and the baby to the Red Cross. You know, Quaid actually tried feeding the baby goat milk but couldn't milk the goat! So he screams, 'Don't any of the tits in this country work!' That was funny, you know? But then, she accepts the kid and feeds it. She is now looking for a bus to take them to, wherever…to the Red Cross camp. And Quaid is waiting for her with the baby. Quaid's going to die in the end."

"Why?"

"That's how it always is."

"Isn't it violent? Should you be watching this stuff?"

"No, I shouldn't. I should be watching *The Pink Panther*. Or the *Titanic*. But I called for it and you know how I cannot stop watching a movie once I start. What time is your flight? I packed your things. Most of them."

"I have to leave before 4:30."

"Will you help yourself to dinner? I could serve you!"
"I'll get it."

He took a moment too long to answer. He will sleep soon. She will finish the movie alone. Later.

She joins him at the table with the popcorn she had prepared for herself, "You better close the deal this time! If you continue the negotiations any more, they may tire of you guys."

 "Tire of us? Why?"

"Things could go wrong."

"Not because they will *tire* of us."

"Not important. The *'how'* is not important. It is the *'what'* that will affect us. Anything could go wrong now that everyone knows what's brewing. It's all over the news. Everyone is hanging on to any straw that they can grab at. As if this one deal will keep the economy afloat."

He understands her now. "Are you referring to the whole evil eye thing? The *nazar* thing."

"It's not a 'thing'."

"Sounds silly coming from a lawyer!" he teases. "Education does not explain the metaphysical."

"Fine. We'll close the deal between tomorrow and the day after. Now can I have some rice?"

She does not like the summary dismissal of her lofty idea but then, that is really all she had to say.

*　　*　　*

– I am glad he is leaving. I will have two days and two nights to myself. He'll be too busy to call. Not different from how it has been of late but the geography makes it…tangible. A holiday from the mundane. I will not miss him. Don't let him sense this, though…

I will act on all those little plans one saves up for a day spent alone. Things that you cannot plan to do, silly things like a walk along Marine Drive, to see the sun set, on a weekday!

A walk along the filthy streets of this city to nowhere in particular…

A ride in the bus to wherever its last stop is…

And back. –

They did that once, she smiles remembering. They took a train from the Victoria Terminus to Panvel, dined at a restaurant there and took the last train back to the city. She had spoken endlessly about college and he had been quietly interested.

– we don't do that now. We have moved on to a more settled, less exuberant state, the state of marriage. But I am not sad. I *need* these two days, now. Been more scatterbrained than usual. I haven't had enough time and space to think my thoughts through…–

*   *   *

"What will you do while I am away?"

"Mope around, waiting for you to return."

He smiles. "Are you going out with Deb?"

Does he know that she is looking forward to him going away?

– no. I don't want Debbie. I want to be alone. –

He helps her clear the table.

"I will miss you, and you know that."

He ruffles her hair and kisses her head forgiving her. He is treating her like a child again. Suddenly, she is irritated with the uncanny tenderness – a little like incest.
She stands at the door watching him settle down to sleep. He looks at her, "I've set the alarm. You shouldn't wake up. I'll sneak out. Now go finish your movie."

She smiles at his sweet dismissal, setting out his suit for the morning while he watches her from his cozy perch. "Want to thank me for doing this for you?" she says.

"Yes. Come, let me cuddle you!"

"No. Thanks!" She returns to watching, *Savior*.

*   *   *

– oh no.

The mother is singing that lullaby that all the women, Serbs and Bosnians, in that country seem to sing for their babies. Nee-Ne-No-Ne-Naa-Ne…

Cliché.

I don't fall for this sort of thing. They are not the same, they may sing the same songs to their babies but they are driven with a primitive emotion. Primitive emotion. I picked that up from one of the Star Trek episodes.

She is singing the lullaby really loudly for the baby who is with Quaid. Her bus has been stopped by armed men, very close to the boathouse in which Quaid and the baby are hiding.

Cannot watch this…I hope the singing keeps Baby quiet…Quaid cannot fight all these men! Even if he is a US soldier or whatever. Or is he a Frenchman? Was Stellan Skarsgård also French? What's happening?

These armed men are smashing everybody's heads one by one. Near a lake, or pond. Quaid's taking aim but the Mother shakes her head at him. No.

So this fat man takes aim with a sledgehammer and just hits people's heads…lets them drop in the pond. No one even bothers begging to be spared. She sings…Nee-Ne-No-Ne-Naa-Ne…

Mass graves! Mass graves…Her singing's stopped. The Mother…

Did they kill her? God! I can't take this anymore.

Get a drink of water…let it run while you get it…you won't miss much.

Yes. That's her pink coat. She's face down in the water and bobbing. She is dead. She is dying. It cannot be in an instant, no?

Bloody hell! Tears. This is it. I am crying. Nice flick.

Am I to be satisfied with Quaid and Baby making it to the Red Cross? Did they really do this to people?

*   *   *

Dennis Quaid calls the Baby *his* daughter. And is smiling at the stranger woman from the bus that he finally boarded with the Baby. The stranger woman sings the same lullaby…Nee-Ne-No-Ne-Naa-Ne… –

*   *   *

She brushes her teeth.

– let the tears drop…I can feel them well up past the rims of my lower eyelids.

The lower lids are a dam that will be breached…

There! It can contain them no more.

Feel them spill over and stream down the cheeks, taking two courses – one along the sides of my nose touching the sides of my lips, which will open to their salty taste and the other, along my cheekbone down my neck…

Even bordering my ears, wetting my earlobes when I lie down.

Shall I speak with me? Calm me down?

I whisper, "Why are you crying?"

Cry some more.
He is sleeping.

I can still see those images.

Sledgehammers slamming their heads. So simple. That simple.

Like cracking walnuts. That simple.

Isn't it wonderful that I can see things when what I am actually looking at is the pillow? The bed?

It is the kind of profound observation that puts people off…too busy to notice…too wound up to do anything about such things…these are things you learn to take for granted…of course, you can see the images! You have a mind, don't you? We all see images. We are all cameras...what a childlike, idiotic thing to stop and ponder about.

to her great works did Nature link, the human soul that through me ran...

Longfellow? Wordsworth? No. Longfellow...Kingsley used it in the *Water Babies...*

and much it grieved my heart to think, what man has made of man...
Should I read something? Change of mood?

No.

My eyes are tired. Kill the crying. It is so tiring. If I want to see him off...better sleep now.

Not *'great'* works. To her *'fair'* works did Nature link...the human soul that...blah...

Sleep...great works...fair works...same difference!

So the baby was saved and Quaid did not die. But everyone else did.

What happened to happy endings? –

26/11/2008, 2 A.M.

*two men with machine guns? standing on a hill, their guns
know the target - me.*
no effort at all. shooting away –
RAT-A-TAT-TAT-TAT-TAT-TAT.
 constant, scary, deafening gunfire against…
a log cabin?
have to find my way in. one door in the front…
only way in, only way out
*I could nearly be there. must be alert. bullets barely missing
me,*
getting locked in the wood –
*DHAG-DHAG-DHAG-DHAG-DHAG-DHAG-DHAG-
DHAG*
*chasing me, chasing me. I am desperate, so desperate to get
through that one door. Inside the cabin…*
I am going to make it. wait! wait! I cannot die!
the verandah is bordered with a wood railing.
*the 'L', gives me an angle, a vertex. shelter. But I cannot
remain here,*
I am so close to that door. have to get in.
incessant rounds of fire focused at my feeble shelter.
DHAG-DHAG-DHAG-DHAG-DHAG

if I move, they will get me.
if I don't move the bullets will wear down the wood to finish me
DHAG-DHAG-DHAG-DHAG-DHAG!
louder than ever, in my face, in my head. NO! NO!
I must pray. Oh GOD! please help me! pray! pray! pray! PRAY! help me!
it is happening, it is happening…the magic.
I am becoming small.
smaller and smaller, everything about me is bigger and bigger and the sounds, louder.
I am as small as an ant.
they don't see me running across the few feet to that door.
gunfire still targeted at the vertex-shelter…
cannot see me! cannot see me!
I am running that short distance, now become great because I am so little…
so close! so close!
I am through! past that door! through the air gap between the door and the floor!
I fooled them. I fooled them…

*   *   *

– nightmares have happy endings.

I should be used to this one now. It has been repeating itself since as long as I can remember being able to dream.

Or since as long as I can remember being able to remember my dreams…

Is it a dream, or a nightmare?

No fun trying to give death a miss even if you do make it in the end.

It's a nightmare.

But you have to make it in the end. You don't dream your own death.
Only 2:15.
Long way to go. Will I sleep again?

He sleeps so soundly. Does he dream like I do?

When did I learn about gunfire? And guns? How could I know that *sound*? Did they let me see violent flicks as a kid…the sound is from the movies, isn't it?

Can you dream about things you don't know? How far can imagination get you?

> *'Touch yourself, take a hot shower,*
> *pint of beer and knock off…'*
> *her perfect Sunday afternoon,*
> *'Better than the real thing, Babes!' JD winks at us*
eager listeners.

Where is JD now? Does she still resort to a little DIY? She was putting on an act. I am certain now. Her winking was not spontaneous nor was the accompanying grinning. She'd probably practiced it in the bathroom mirror that morning. Too good to be real. No one is that cool...She was a difficult roommate. Too alert to all my actions. Even when she slept, JD would ask me to stop talking to myself. I couldn't ever think of anything smart to say. That would have made her back the hell off.

Heartbeat's faster than usual.

They never hit me. If they did, I would wake up, starting at being shot at.

But I would not die.

I'd recreate the dream. I would find the snag that makes it impossible for me to die. Like discovering that the shot hadn't hit any of the vital organs, or that the shooters fell off the cliff in spite of their perfectly balanced, parted-leg stance. Superman would come for me. Something would save me. Something would happen. Not death.

Are we in a desert? Do you dream in colours? Or don't you? What is it that they say? This one has a brownish-yellow, sepia hue.

Death, be not proud! Hogwash...
And why not?
It's a job well done,
See! Dark clouds!
I snatch away,

Leaving you in tears -
Why should I, Death, not be proud?

Write that down! Keep writing instruments handy. When will I learn? I will have forgotten the lines by morning.

Forgotten them already. Must try to sleep. –

*   *   *

Frank Hardy. Straight out of the Hardy Boys' Casefiles
Dark hair. Dark eyed, Frank.
He kisses me
Passionately
I am Callie Shaw…
It's going slow, real slow, because we want to take our time…
No.
He looks like Frank Hardy. His name is Frank Hardy.
But he is a gallant officer from centuries past
And I, a damsel in distress
A feisty damsel, ahead of her times, in distress
Who he has rescued…in more ways than he knows
She is his faithful servant and loves him ardently never letting
him guess.
From a distance…
till one night he finds the door to her room ajar and enters
He sees her in a flowing white night dress
She does not know how much
her image framed by the doorway to
the moonlit terrace affects him…
and no, there is in fact a storm coming…
cut the moonlit terrace…

it's a dark night, actually
lightening, flashes…a roll of thunder…
the wind…
Her loose flowing hair, which he has only seen tied up in a
severe knot…
Catches the wind like the sails of a hapless ship at sea…
She hurriedly turns to close the doors
he rushes to help her…
they touch
lightening
why did he not see this?
Her head is bowed
He needs to know
He touches her chin
Lifts her face
And sees the want in her blue eyes
His touch is electrifying
He knows that he is home
an enrapturing trance now
she always stood at the precipice
all it takes is a touch
her knees are weak, she falls…
He holds her,
she clings to his broad chest
He gathers her tresses, pulls her head back, her lips parted
He caresses her neck, discovers her breasts,
each touch is a revelation
Kissing, nuzzling, flushed sighing…
Passionate…
Passionate love-making

settling in on a resigned rhythm
to a primitive beat…
till…
it happens
Because it must…
Wild…uncontrollable…insatiable…
They hold each other then, tiredly reliving it all…and deep
sleep envelopes them…

*   *   *

– Oh, well. At least I am yawning now.
One thing that I do know for sure is this: I will be a pathetic writer of erotica. Do not give me credit for a thousand wet dreams and men jerking off.
The man in my dreams. Is always, Frank.

The importance of being Frank.

Frank Hardy. Women drool about that sort of name. Like Captain Kirk.

Frank vs Joe Hardy, you know? *Frank. Ernest.* The importance of the name.
Joe Hardy had his moments but was all brawn and Frank was the brain…that is what appeals to women.
Frank Hardy. If someone really had that name, I would be his Callie Shaw. Dark hair and brown eyes help too.
Clearly, the guys – all those ghost writers – that created him preferred Frank themselves.

Huge crush that I haven't gotten over. What if I told anyone about it?

They wouldn't understand. They'd think it weird and juvenile.

They'd think that you were being cute.

It *is* weird.

Yes. But that doesn't matter because it is your little secret.

It will die with me.

I've not seen anyone dead yet…unless you count the movies and newspapers. When Baba died, I was a kid…

Didn't go for the funeral. Exam or something.

Were they protecting me? Didn't want me to see it?

Death.

I know what it can do, though. Dadda refused to leave their house saying that she wanted to die there, right there, where he went from. I did not cry soon enough when I heard the news…what was everyone doing? I can remember only the somberness of it all.

I miss the thought of him now. I would have known him some more. Do the older cousins remember? Did he share serious Grandfatherly wisdom with them? Say memorable things? For us, he had danced. We had laughed. –

*   *   *

he rests his left hand on his waist, in the 'I'm-a-tea-pot pose';
his right hand sits on top of his head
he goes round and round
and he moves his hips, swaying them with purposeful clumsiness
exaggerated also - I now see - with the heaviness of age

– was it so funny? Why did we laugh? Why is it not funny anymore?

I dread death. Not just my own, everyone's.

A fear magnified with time. Age kills.

First, you lose your innocence.

Starting with knowledge of life processes, the systems of the body, peristalsis and reverse peristalsis.

The whole puberty thing - sudden hair in wrong places. And the slowly definite progression towards being that adult you naively fantasize about becoming.
Lots of hugs and kisses through the milestones - at thirteen, at sixteen, at eighteen. Twenty-one.

You know what's wrong with it all? It isn't just the whole physical development, figuring the differences of the genders out and all that and frigging life processes.

It is the *total* loss of innocence. And we're not talking snakes and apples here. No, Sir, I'm thinking, the growing-up.

Real stuff, expectations, the far future, beyond the next minute, the next hour or tomorrow. Retirement plans. Life insurance. Careers. Earning your bread. Survival. Yes. I know. Yes, they call it, 'maturity'.

Jealousy beyond rivalry.

Anger beyond irritability.

Impatience beyond tantrums.

Imprudence beyond child play.

Intolerance beyond hatred.
Propriety beyond good behaviour.

Etiquette beyond good manners.

Understanding beyond comprehension.

You cannot argue that kids have worries of their own. You get flogged on sheer scales here given the very simple, overt, uninhibited requirements of a child.

A kid knows who the guys most likely to succumb to a tantrum are. This insight dies with age. We want it all. Want to get away with having it all. And we don't know how to ask for it. We kill. Murder. Hurt. Blow up each other. We can think about it. Wish someone dead.

Like pure baby's breath turning putrid because she grew teeth.

Can I enjoy a thunderstorm with the wind trapped in the trees, late, late at night? With nothing worrying me because it is summer vacation.

And witness a hail storm, diving out from under the porch to collect icicles that immediately melt in my mouth?

Can I read late into the night because it doesn't matter when I will wake up in the morning? Because the night is a vast ocean of possibility.

Can this reading happen in the old house in Dehra Dun, surrounded with the wilderness of the cantonment and the startling call of the *titeeri* occasionally breaking the wild, sleeping silence?

Can I laugh about why I prefer the Hindi name, *titeeri*, to the 'Red-wattled Lapwing' because of that metaphor that we learnt in school about it sleeping on its back with its legs in the air and how this still wouldn't hold the heavens up? *Titeeri se aasmaan thama jayega?*[1]

---

[1] Will the lapwing be able to hold the heavens up?

Back then I could enjoy metaphors on the futility-of-it-all without ever suspecting that they could also make me cry…

Can I be as wise as a serpent and as innocent as a dove?

I am wise. I know who's flirting with me and I could flirt back.

I know which Partners in the Firm cannot stand my face and I know that even if they know that I know this, they don't care. They don't have to care.

I know that when you don't like somebody you don't just stick your tongue out at them and let them go figure.

No. Instead, you're civil. You will make a joke or two and speak to them about the latest flicks, great restaurants.

The games that we play are contrived with consequences more severe than 'who will be the next den'.

Climate change, terrorist attacks, crimes against women, taxes, corruption.

I am the serpent. I want to be a dove.

Everything, everyone is old around me, I am never going to be ready to let go.

I WANT PERPETUAL *STATUS QUO*!

Oh God! I will not be ready. I will be so overwhelmed. I will go mad, mad, mad, mad, mad.

I should die. Take me before anyone else! That is the solution. I'll watch over them then, protect them. I'll come back for them. Let them lose me rather than I, them.

How will he react? He won't remarry.

He'll isolate himself. No new friends. He will drink occasionally with the old ones, he will cry sometimes.

He will drink alone.

He'll be alone, but that is alright.

Get back to sleep, freak! Stop weeping! No one died! Get a grip.

Get a grip.

2:45 A.M. Running out of time.

Shall I hug him?

No.

Don't disturb him. He may even push you away.

I'll just look at him... –

*   *   *

I can fly.

> *when I really need to,*
> *I can lift off the ground in a twirl. With a little more-than-usual focus...*

> *we are in the mansion in Rasoolabad, massive rooms and high ceilings*
> *I hear them gossiping*
> *the scandal and the affair*
> *They see me behind the sofa...*
> *They chase me...angry*
> *I dodge them all*
> *I am laughing with nervous rancor telling them that I will tell...*
> *They are angry, they will hurt me...they will shut me up*
> *Too many hands reaching for me...grabbing at my legs, my shoulders...*

> *I have to fly...now!*
> *I lift off the ground and I flutter near the high ceiling...*
> *Look at their faces...they are gaping...I laugh and laugh and laugh.*
> *Something's not right...*
> *There is this nervous edge to their expressions,*

my laughter…everything

I levitate gaining the momentum of your average bird rising in small circles
I see the tops of trees,
we're being chased. we are fast but it's catching up with us.

green grass. there is grass, hills and trees. blue skies.
the city's skyline.
telecom towers and skyscrapers.
I cannot run faster than this.
take my hand. don't be scared! don't look back…

I move my spare arm - you cannot call it flapping - like a wounded wing.
and we're off the ground! flying. small circles. too low! it could still get us.
wave harder, wave harder…up-down, up-down, deeper, concerted movement.
we soar! leaving it shocked, defeated.
over the city, swooping past the skyscrapers
like it is the most obvious thing to do,
we're flying…

*   *   *

– awake again.

Heart racing. Achieved the impossible!

Hands shaking. Adrenalized breathing.

This is not the Superman kind of flying. No.

It is surer than that. The aviation of birds. Such a sense of power!

3:15 A.M. Forty-five minutes to go.

Must sleep. Move closer to him.–

26/11/2008, 4 A.M.

She watches the clock crawl its way to triggering the buzzer, suffering the forced wakefulness from her visions of genocidal sledgehammers smashing helpless heads, giving way to the nightmares, cold sweat and strange thoughts intermingled with worrying memory. She turns off the buzzer a second before it goes off.

– I should have called for something light. *The Pink Panther*. Not bloody *Savior*. Should've Googled for spoilers.

But when I read about a movie, I develop affection for it.

Like falling in love with being in love.

Which is why I sat through *Mrs. Dalloway*. –

She rolls over to her side, nice and easy. He needn't wake up yet.

She wished that he'd put the toothpaste in the ceramic mug she had bought. She finds it on the second shelf above the basin, a comfortable height for him but she has to stretch to reach it.

– hmmm, bleeding gums.–

The light coolness of an early morning breeze distracts her.

– the only time, other than the monsoons, when Bombay is tolerable.

What was that poem? Did it in class 9 or 10, a chapter of poems on the subject of 'morning'.

He likens the morning breeze to his mother waking him up. She smells of the flowers that she carries in her tray…or does she wear them in her hair?

She runs cool hands, fresh from her bath, gently over his forehead. He thinks of his mother when the morning breeze wakes him. Touching his forehead with its cool coolness.

How helpless you feel when you forget something that you remember.

A simple poem. I like simple poems. With some *anupras alankar* thrown in for effect.

I like alliteration.

Hah! But this morning breeze can't fool me for long. It smells of dead fish. Faint stench. The uptightness of this neighbourhood does not deceive me, it stinks alright. –

*　　*　　*

She lays her light shawl on him. She could stand here staring at him for hours.

– or a few long minutes, at least.

I could stay awake, just to hear you breathing… –

He snores. She smiles. Get the coffee ready.

The mawkish state is a killer. She does not have time for the tears blurring her vision. He is awake now, she hears him shuffling towards the kitchen. He knows she's being stupid but says nothing.

– thank God. –

He hugs her, leaning heavily on her like he's dozed-off again, and she has to laugh, 'Go away! You'll miss your flight!'

*　　*　　*

She stands alone in the kitchen. She will miss him.

"Coffee's ready!"

"Yah! Coming!"

He's slipping into the carefully ironed trousers that she had laid out for him last night. He cannot understand her passion for 'straightening' clothes out even when they are back from the *dhobi* but she has to rid them of the unnecessary creases where they were folded – that mark of the washerman's trade.

She watches him drink his coffee. He focuses on yesterday's paper. She can usually hold the tears back but they just won't stop today.

He is looking for his wallet. He will leave soon. Quick hug.

She sees him disappear around the corner and hears him take the stairs till she finds herself listening to the silence.

– I can still hear him… no.

Not anymore. –

*　　　*　　　*

Meera stands at the door looking at the hollow passageway of shut doors.

– the cold aloofness of a person who is sleeping. All wrapped up in himself. He would be startled into a disapproving coherence if you woke him.

A sleeping person doesn't want to be disturbed. Nor I!

I don't feel so bad anymore! This is what I wanted. I feel light! And excited!

So much to do! And it will all be done! –

She looks for a pen to list her plan for the day but just sits at her desk instead, staring into the dark morning.

– I am vain if I think that I beat the Sun.

No lists! There are way too many things to do and it has to be spontaneous. I don't want to set goals and targets and deadlines and then appraise my performance. That is exactly what I am revolting against today.

Or maybe the things I want to do are too few to bother listing? No. It has to be spontaneous, not tied to…a list. That's all.

A conscious effort to go with the flow. –

I am a writer. my pen, poised, ready to write what swarms my mind.
the only thing stopping me is the presence of a second person in the room…
and constant loquacity

the writer who did not call for silence is alone,

his desk waits with a welcoming blank sheet of excellent yellow
ruled paper
a fountain pen – the writer's particular preference – with full
tank invites him lovingly
to pick it up and gratify his longing to begin, and finish, his
prose, his verse.

I am writing to finish what I began...
I can hear the pen scratch the paper...
the scrubbing sound of great and uncontrollable passion...

– no. –
I'm the artist.
my brush is heavy with colour,
poised to dash off all the inspiration
stifling my mind.
ravish that ready, chaste canvas...
it will take form now...

– no. I am a firecracker, ready to explode and shoot out
a thousand sparkles! But first, let me languish in bed to
miss him some more, wait for his call, say goodbye once
more. –

CHAPTER 2
MORNING

The car alarm that goes off every morning to the accompaniment of an unsynchronized choir of crows wakes her up. It is 8 A.M.

– Did I sleep that long?

Two missed calls. From him.

Shall I sleep some more?

What a waste that would be!

– missed saying bye, but what the heck! I am looking forward to…to my bath this morning. Rearing to go.

Is it possible to look forward to the mundane?

Could it not be mundane…for a day?
If you lived every minute of your life, not involuntarily acting because you had to, but consciously experiencing it, every minute, yes…

One could look forward to a bath, even if one had had one just last evening.

Shall I brush my teeth? Given that I did brush earlier...this morning?

Or surrender to the affirmative urge instead of arguing with myself on the principle of the thing? –

*   *   *

Meera puts on the *Vedic Chants* CD that she had purchased for when the fetus had fully developed hearing capabilities.

– you like to begin your day with something spiritual. Radio is too secular now to play such stuff. Or one or two channels that are embarrassingly Hindu very early in the morning...when no one listens.

They could do a mix like the *Sarva Dharma Prathana* that we did in school...
every Friday, the assembly read a common theme or subject from the primary religious texts.

But a school, a good private one, can enforce ideologies without bothering about public opinion.

If they did something like that on Radio, a hundred people would stand up saying that one or the other hymns or prayers or whatever was offensive. Or that more Hindu *bhajans* played or too many Muslim ones and not enough Christian ones.

Why court controversy?

Give them all instead, a morning filled with the irksome, frivolous chatter of radio jockeys and numbers on love and life, and lust.

No inhibited sense of propriety, no hiding behind the flowing long skirts of lyricism, no skirting the issue.

The singer's intentions are clear from the start – *let me hold you, come caress my body, you got me going crazy…*you *turn me on! Turn me on!*

Unpleasant morning listening. –

*   *   *

She takes her time in the shower.

– what emotion does the stream of hot water down your back elicit?

Does relaxing equal happiness?

I want to get past the quotable quotes and one-liners on posters and T-shirts and all.

Just to figure it out, not define it. *Know* it. Then I won't miss it when I pass it by.

a ride on the bike late at night, no…
early in the morning,
when the city that never sleeps can't help dozing,
just after the last lot of party goers has driven home
just before the early-birds wake up.
That vacuum when you free fall because you are out so late and so early,
because it is night and also day,
even the cops don't know if they should bother with you…

It cannot be everlasting. No more than a few minutes. A moment, just a moment that could spread over time, but a moment all the same. Fleeting.

We never know the exact moment we're happy at.

Then, you look back and you say, 'Hey! That was a happy time!'

Those were the BEST days of my life! The shower is happiness.

Elemental purity that blankets my nakedness against the chill, bringing me together in pieces, going slowly over the fragments that are out in the cold, cajoling them to join in its warm hug. –

*　　　*　　　*

She could call in sick, take the day off. But a part of today's freedom is just that, 'Making the system work for me, not breaking with routine, just trying to fit life into it!' She will flit in and out. They will not bother with her because, well, she has been working too hard.

*　　　*　　　*

we play seven-tiles in the park next to the house...
The three-ton stops outside the gate
Its camouflage is not the routine solid-olive-green but the patchy woodland camouflage...

its dark inside looks hollow.
Till we discern eyes staring out at us, for a second,
only many gleaming eyes,
then we make out shapes inside this truck
those eyes belong to faces, still indiscernible.
we move closer wondering why it had stopped in front of our quarters.
From the darkness inside, he emerged, first his beret, then the face looking out and down at us and then, the rest of him, stooped over because of the low canvas roof, emerging from amidst the limbs that the three-ton was dropping home.
He was back from Sri Lanka!
He brought me a red Walkman.
We had shouted in amazed glee for Mummy!

– the surprised joy of meeting again. –
he looked at us again, and again, and kept telling us that we were taller.

We boasted about school. Mummy cooked.
He stayed a few days making most of the time,
One of the officers in the colony had died last month. He was
a Captain. We had visited the family.
A young woman had sat in a daze. Unblinking. That had
worried me.

Would they kill you?
He had said, 'No'.
But they had killed that young Captain…

– I cannot remember the name. They had lived in the
block opposite ours. –

he told us about the Geneva Convention
he showed us the Red Cross on his uniform
I loved the Red Cross on the white circle after that…
it would protect us…

– those days are a blur. Just that moment, those few
minutes that I can remember.

The precise instantaneity of happiness.

What does he remember from those days? I should ask
him the next time we speak.
We live too much in the present. –

*   *   *

She turns around to face the shower, reveling in the streams starting at her forehead, and the straight lines that follow the contours - now substantial - of her body. Some of these streams merge with other straight lines that cannot run parallel anymore, some streams reach her feet and the floor, unwavering in their path, tributaries to the larger flow of water that springs along the scarred and indented marble floor circling in on the gaping drain, to drop some distance so that the drain joins in the shushing of the shower with a comforting drip-dripping-gurgling of its own.

She is startled out of her meditation with something, or someone, stroking her back.

– a hand! It was! It was! All palm and fingers… –

She knew it! She has known all along! They were trying to get to her…the ghosts.

The old landlady had mentioned that her sick husband had died and that this toilet was the one he had used during his sickness…
– which explained its weird design. What is the landlady's name? Cannot remember.–

She had wondered what the old lady meant when she had told them, 'My husband was a sick man'.

– an odd choice of words it had been. Was he just ill? Or was he sick, also in the head? –

She was sure he haunted this house.

– it wasn't a natural death, right? He is still around. He is trying to connect with me. I have always felt this thing, this…presence. –

*   *   *

She reaches for her towel. She did not bring it in. She darts out of the toilet, forgetting to turn off the shower, avoiding looking at the mirror that has fogged up and from where she is sure that she is being stared at. She has to hurry, and be careful.

– no accidents! No accidents!

They are in the mirrors because a fraction of the soul stays behind with the reflection. Mirrors have memory. A reflection is magical. Unlike a photograph that only captures images and casts them in time with the flashing of the camera's shutter. A mirror captures the moment and also its passing. You age before the mirror and it sees that happening, right then…you don't want to see what it sees…the mirror makes a memory of its own, and when you die, you come back to those mirrors to look for what you had missed…wondering why you had missed it…and to stare out at the world…to scare the world…or to connect with it…

Shit scared of mirrors…

No accidents. Be careful.

Where did I leave my towel? –

*   *   *

Near panic, she wraps herself as she rushes towards the main door, dripping wet. People would hear her scream, if she did, but would they react? Or would she be like that stupid car alarm that goes off each morning? No one would bother. They were all so old and foggy, so deaf. She could not scream even if she tried.

– I can think…I am thinking…I haven't lost it…I am not mad…I can think…

Where is my voice? I cannot hear myself…people…I need people…

But you cannot step out naked!

I won't. But I will get to that door and open it. I have to show the Presence that I have access to my own world.

It scares them off…I think! *Hope.* –

*   *   *

She pulls at the door, her moist hand slipping at the handle. It slams open, making her jump.

She peeps into the hallway that had greeted her so shabbily earlier this morning.

Not much has changed except, to her relief, that a maid stands at the door on the left, waiting to be answered.

She looks at the maid, then turns to look over her shoulder into her silent house, her wet footprints gleaming in the morning light from the living-room window.

She peeps out again to find that the woman is looking at her...with no expression at all.

The woman shows neither surprise, nor disdain, nor anything worth writing about, in response to a near naked woman, fresh out of her bath slamming the door to her house open, and staring at her.

*   *   *

Meera stands at the threshold, conscious of the maid with the poker face till she feels herself calming down.

– this is what a blank stare looks like. This is what it means - deadpan expression. She has nothing to look forward to and little to look back on.

Her dreary existence in the slum that the seawater floods during the monsoon and the sun burns down upon in the summer and the fact that she cleans for the tired, retired, deaf, almost dead, residents of Colaba has been opium for her senses.

She is beaten at home and sees her kids given similar treatment by her drunken lout of a husband.

She is numb. She does not cry anymore and sometimes she uses really vulgar abuses for her tormentor, his parents and sisters, only to get hit back into silence.

Her children listen, imbibing their inheritance.

She does not react to stimuli, or to semi-naked, dripping wet, pregnant women standing furtively at their doors…at a quarter to ten in the morning.

I am obliged to her for being here.

I should tell her that she can call me the next time the man hits her and that I would help her organize an effective socking of his liquor-swollen convoluted face, but she will not ask for help.

She does not know what that means. She is numb.

I leave it at that. –

She gives the lifeless woman a last grateful look and warily turns back into the haunted house, closing the door on the deserted corridor. She continues to stand at the threshold, conscious of the maid with the poker face till she feels herself calming down.

26/11/2008, 10:15 A.M.

Her bell-bottomed maternity trousers are too long for her. She holds them up so that the cuffs don't sweep the street but flap irritatingly at her ankles.

– I hate Colaba. Its grumpy, monopolistic shopkeepers, aged standalone badly lit ill-maintained residential apartments that we pay a king's ransom for. The cranky domestic help who forget that they live in a stinky slum. –

"Starved for choice," she mutters as she walks in her comfortable shoes, ignoring the taxi stand and its waiting cabs. She is sure that no cabby will take her to Ballard Estate because it is 'too close'.

This daily impertinence of the cabbies troubles her.
– one, they are way too low down the socio-economic ladder to be so holding me at ransom.

Two, they provide an 'essential' service for the provision of which they were issued a license and are not *allowed* to refuse to execute this service.

Three, Ballard Estate is more than twice the basic fare away and it is not therefore 'too close'.

Four, since I started showing, I had expected some decency, respect for an expectant lady, which I haven't received because they are scum. –

She waits for an empty cab across the taxi stand. The vain cabbies with vacant cabs at the taxi stand ignore her as studiously as she ignores them. She curses them with accidents, trouble with cops, and what not.

Everyone likes to screw with a cabby. And auto-rickshaw drivers.

She has a plan. Today, she will have her revenge.

Her heart thumps with excitement, waiting for the next empty taxi that she will hail.

Word will spread. They will all follow her example. A revolution! Justice!
– where are the cabs! I'm waiting, I'm waiting.

Keep a straight face! Don't let them suspect anything.

Of course. –

*   *   *

She spots her target emerging from the washer-men's gully. She will be his first customer, the *boni*, the first piece of wealth that the Goddess bestows in the hands of tradesmen, and which income the cabbies shun with shameful alacrity.

– let him *not* be a sincere man!

Give me this chance to teach them all a lesson! –

She hails the cab. He slows down just enough to hear her destination.

– this is my man.

He's retaining the option to accelerate and be off if he thinks I want to go to a place that is 'too close'. –

He has to stop because the buses are honking for him to move or get out of their way.

– perfect.
You do that. Keep your foot on the accelerator and your ears cocked for the name of my destination…My man, alright! –

She does a half-squat-forward-lunge to peep into the cab informing him, with a straight face that she wants to go to Ballard Estate. He shakes his head in refusal starting to drive away but stops when she asks if he will go to Bandra.

"Yes, but what about Ballard Estate?"

She has only to pick up a file that will be delivered to her in the cab, so he will not have to wait for more than a minute.
He says, "Okay".

She watches her victim in the rear view mirror. He doesn't suspect a thing.

– he thinks he is going to make a hundred and fifty bucks off me when he gets me to Bandra. But, I am not going to Bandra. An adventure. Is happiness…–

*   *   *

With her mind so focused on the plan and how it would best play out, she forgets to cover her nose as she passes the *Macchi Maar Nagar* slum, which throws up a stink any time of the day and must destroy the existence of the residents of Badhwar Park, with all that fish drying in the hot sun.
The bamboo matrix and the fish dangle-drying on it was a sort of flag. It explained the boat-house-slum-village, the hundreds of colourful, small boats bobbing on the ocean.

The taxi in front has been hired by fisherwomen. Its boot is loaded with fresh stock for the market. She notices the crow riding on the boot waiting patiently for it to be opened. Waiting to grab a bite.

– beautiful black bird. Intelligent. Its beauty undermined. They call him ugly. Not as stately as the raven, but cute. Dark eyes, deep. Wise.

He will be judged.

He knows that you squirm at his food, at his not-pretty cawing.

No one listens to his other voices. He gurgles, if you let him.

Nobody knows of the bravery with which a single crow nudges the eagle away, matching the eagle's ascent, bit by bit, as the larger bird flies higher and higher trying desperately to throw him off until the eagle surrenders into seeking other hunting grounds.

The black bird returns to its lair on a rooftop of silent crows who have been watching...too honorable to join in the fight, too quiet to have been uninterested…

Why does he do this? Is it vultures or eagles? What reason for such constant animosity? I don't know.

No one studies the brilliant architecture of his nest.

It hasn't the classical feel of the tailor and weaver birds' nests.

It could be a *Howard Roark* construction. It's not on Animal Planet or National Geographic when I watch…

A triangular fortress of a pile of straight sticks
centred on a soft circular hollow of tender dried twigs.
It could be a pagan symbol for something…the circle in a triangle

their strong beaks
have ripped the thick stems of the magnificent palm at my window.
They need neither camouflage nor clutter.

They caw rudely in loud panic at everybody except me.
We have to keep the window shut.
I am special

She clutches tightly at her bag. Her hands are moist. Accelerated heartbeat. The traffic is closing us down. I have more time…

I scream for him to come to the window
The crows' nest has eggs!
Blue, white, grey…patchy, like pebbles on the floor of a waterfall.
He says, 'How can such an ugly bird be born of such beautiful eggs?'
I am not angry he called them ugly, everyone says that.
I put my palm on the pane as guarantee that there will be no danger from us.

He has gone back to reading the paper.
Is the unlikely bird that has built its home in ours a sign of things to come…?

He sees the baby birds hatch out of the eggs shouting for me to come and see!
The crows are mad with fury
I look at the translucent bodies of their babies…
And recoil unnerved, 'So ugly!'
Then, angry that I said that, I scream for him to step away from the window

Over the next few days the babies die
it wasn't a sign for me…
just nature taking its course, like it does with birds and animals…
The crows still mope around in the empty nest
The female even buffers the loosening triangular fortress sometimes.
they screech at me now
they think I took their babies.

I can feel the fetus shifting, moving, but cannot see the movement, yet
He works on an Excel sheet in the white, blue light of his notebook.
I think, 'Maybe the babies were cuckoos?'
Type-tapping keys…
Not listening…

'You know, a cuckoo lays its eggs in the crow's nest…?'

He smiles, not looking at me, type-tapping, glowing in the white, blue light,
'Yes. Maybe...'

*   *   *

The taxi is passing the Reserve Bank of India buildings now and Ballard Estate is close. She is calm.
I laugh a mirthless laugh...

– no.

The laugh is too much. I hope he doesn't relent easily! I want to tell him a thing or two. So he can carry the message... –

With a scornful smile on my face I say, 'So? How does it taste? Your own medicine?'

– no. No, again.

How do you say that in Hindi? The 'taste your own medicine' bit? He wouldn't understand... –

I say, 'Tell your cabby friends, this is how Mumbai works now... you don't do your job, we MAKE you do it.'

– hmmm! Much better! –

She directs him to stop near the building that houses her office and gets out, half-squats to look directly at the driver and asks, "How much?"

He loses his composure, and asks about the Bandra destination piece.

Studiously ignoring the question, she reaches for the cash in her purse. She takes these reluctant cabs every day. She knows what the tab is.

He builds on his grumbling theme. He would never have agreed to the *savari* had he known that this is where she had wanted to come to. It is 'too close'.

This is her cue.

She raises her head from the depths of her purse, having scrounged for exact change.

She speaks in an even voice, "Yes. I know you wouldn't have come. That is why I took the trouble to fool you. This is how it is going to be from now on. You refuse to do your job we will *make* you do it!"

> *my audience is applauding.*
> *I hear cheering*
> *Loud cheering…*

With equanimity she puts down the fare on the vacant co-driver's seat.

She ignores his glare as he reaches for the fare so unfairly earned. His work day, they both realize is screwed, at least for now.

She turns haughtily away, like the queen that she should be, holding that big black bag, that suppressive stigma of the educated employee – that slave who hurriedly walks up to his office to take the elevator to his office, sacrificing his will to a cubicle, even if it is the one by the window overlooking the Bombay Port Trust Harbour and yes, it is on the top floor.

*   *   *

She had gloated about her desk at the window for a long time. It was her corner in the world. It was a corner, so she could dream and create, unobserved by anyone. So what if all she created was legal rhetoric based on standard precedents? She had checked the security computers and found that the surveillance cameras did not quite catch this angle. It was comforting to know that they hadn't made it a point to watch her.

– They probably should have…
What am I doing here?

I should quit. Really.

But you cannot! What about the loan?

That's what he will say. And we will fight about why we bought that stupid new house. Did I force him to buy it, like he says I did? –

Her computer takes forever to start. She decides that she will not carry it with her when she leaves the office today.

– too heavy. Won't lug it around. –

*   *   *

'Banker Kills Wife, Children, Two Others, Shoots Self'

The headlines. The story.

She reads it with the voyeuristic attention that this sort of news usually gets.

Her colleagues are in the mood for a midmorning chat. It really is midmorning. She came in only at 11 A.M. But that is alright. Work has been slow.

– don't these idiots see what's happening? They look happy! The world is falling apart, wrapping yourself around yourself will not shelter you from it…ignoring it will not save you from the storm… –

"Did you guys read about the suicide?" she joins in.

Amit had. The others look embarrassed. She wants to hug them and tell them that it was alright if they had not read the paper this morning!

– I am not testing your commitment to the profession, to updating yourself regularly...No. No. I lack that commitment myself. –

Amit, repeats what she knows, "He lost his job. He had mortgaged his house. So he shot his wife and their two kids, his father-in-law, and his sister-in-law, who were just visiting. Then he shot himself. It wasn't just a suicide. Enough murders to make them count more than the fool shooting himself."
"Wow!"

"Where was this?"

"In the U.S. First page news this morning," says Amit, rubbing their noses in it.

Why do people do these things?

He killed his kids!

You cannot decide for third parties whether they are to live or not! A murderer, first.

No, a fool.

"He was obviously out of his mind," she speaks in his defense.

"He had the gun. He obviously planned it."

"Yes. While he was out of his mind…losing it, you know? Maybe he just *had* the gun? Did the papers mention anything about the gun and how he got it?"

"Hey! Hey!" intervenes one of the underdogs, "It happened in the US, why the hell are we so worried about him!" he says smiling that suave smile that could look stupid the next minute.

Now it's her turn to remind him that he should have read the papers, "The family was Indian. The guy was an engineer from IIT-Madras and did his MBA in India. How does it matter that it happened in the US? It is all around, isn't it? We are all sinking. This huge boat, one body. We are all in it and everything affects everyone!"

But then, another colleague joins them and the subject changes to frivolous banter before they return to their desks. She looks at his pictures and those of the once happy family, again.

– something got to him. Poor guy.

Maybe he did not get along with her? He could have just killed himself and left it at that. Why kill them all? Is a likely fall in the standard of life so depressing? Did they argue…fight…just before he did it?

It will send shock waves through their town and the children's school. The killings and the suicide.

Is killing the universal set? Suicide, the sub-set?

To *kill* yourself?

Yep.
Suicide equals form of killing. A more acceptable form of killing. No third parties and all that. –

*   *   *

– he was from the same college as *him*.

My God! Did they know each other?

No, no. This guy was about thirty-five, must've been some years senior... –

He hates her asking him which year he had graduated. Can't she remember the year? It has been repeated as often as she has asked, with increasing impatience.

– I better not ask him again. Was it 1998 or 1994? He isn't that old! We aren't that old! 1996...? –
She cannot remember.

But she remembers the stories he told her about college, the girl he had dated, and that letter that went to his parents.

that is the youth, young, child him. His beard is sparse...

the awkwardly sparse mustache embarrasses him, so he shaves twice a day.
Youthfully lean.
The grass in the college fields did not run wild as it does now.
They had to be outdoors...playing, running against the wind...
I see him running against the wind...
is it windy at all in Chennai?

He frowns in focused concentration at the bowler...his bat ready...the same frown that furrows his forehead when he works...

Late at night they jumped the gates and bicycled to the beach.
Their cycles had been hidden in the shrubs outside the campus that morning. Four of them.
Cycling to the beach, racing each other, racing themselves...

They got so drunk! Smelled like shit...
He is lying on the sand, gazing at the stars that are a nebulous blur.
He hears one of them struggling with reverse peristalsis somewhere near the boats...
Till he is alert, suddenly
one of them has taken off all his clothes
and is running towards the water...
he wakens from his dizzy dreaminess and yells for him to stop!
But the ass keeps on running...so he starts to run too,
a dazed, staggered run...

I am screaming for him not to do this!
But he cannot hear me...because I am not there...

They are all running into the water...

nobody drowns.
they come down with a fever.
the Hostel Warden writes a nasty letter to his parents
detailing his exploits…
They are heroes, for then…

– yes. I can reconstruct him from his old photographs. –

She stares out of the window, smiling.

Her mailbox comes alive. Not much to do except for a query on the Delisting Guidelines.

– these guys just don't give up! –

She smiles reading the challenge that the financial officer of the G***** Group has thrown at her. She loves them for perpetually wanting to 'get-out' or issue more warrants and other assorted instruments to the promoters, and ultimately delist the company. None of this will work unless they go, make that offer to the shareholders that they are supposed to but it means good money for her to keep answering their innovatively silly questions.

*   *   *

Her strained focus on the e-mail loses to the urge to stare outside and daydream. Her eyes wander to a couple perched precariously on the pipes of the opposite building, making their nest.

– which will be of no use to them if they finish their energies defending themselves against imagined enemies instead of looking after the nestlings.

Silly birds! If only they'd focused on providing for their babies rather than screaming at us! The sheer trauma of their stupid voices must've killed the baby crows at my window…–

The building they are making the nest on is the Seafarers' Association office.

– like a government department building reeking of corruption and the callousness of the civil servant…in fact, it could pass for the Income Tax Office. Ha ha…

Whatever happened to the romance and mystique of the seafarer?

The sea is a rare ocean blue all the time at this place. It is usually a crappy, choppy, half-hearted blue, lazy grey, even charcoal black on Marine Drive.

How can they love it? How can they stand its silent acceptance of their consolidated feces?

How can they make out on Marine Drive with it all stinking back at them? –

we are in Rasoolabad, all the cousins…
sitting on the west mosaic stairs,
overlooking the lazy morning flow of the Ganga…

if we look to the left, we see the Ganges appear around the bend,
maintaining its steady flow over the plains,
an older river that has forgotten the riot of its youth when it was the violent Alakhnanda of the Himalayas...
it is now become the tame Ganges on its way to Allahabad...
on the right, further down the bank, is the Ghat where people are bathing...
where they will burn Baba when he dies...
but that doesn't matter because he is sitting with us today,
surrounded with his young blood, listening to their silence and occasional chatter this early morning...

He smiles at our callous jokes, he doesn't interfere when they become obscene...
his poise varies from faintly smiling to deeply pensive...
like us, he is there but not really there...
a gang of young men walks past our wrought-iron gate with tin cans in their hands, 'They are going for a crap!'

they find a spot between our house and the Ghat
pulling up the chequered knee-length towels wrapped around their thin waists,
putting on unabashed display, blackish-brown bottoms, squatting on the sand
and we know why we cannot take a walk along the river...

we are running towards the river now, picking up the soft round pebbles
that the floods last year left for us...

we throw them at the community of defecating young men…
they don't turn to look at us,
we pelt the pebbles at them as we would stray dogs…
they will have to find another spot, later…
they wash themselves and walk away…
they did not wash their hands with soap…
where do the women go?
there are no bushes for miles…just the farms…where we steal
from…

*   *   *

She stares at the mail screaming out its query at her but nothing registers. She knows the individual words, yes, but she cannot remember the preceding word when she moves to the next.

– this won't do. You have to, you *have* to, focus on the thing! –

She starts repeating the words aloud in calling her undisciplined mind to attention.

– no. No, you guys! You cannot delist with the Depository Receipts outstanding. Just do the open offer! –

She will not respond right away. She'll mull over it. Look at the Code again. Touch the SEBI Manual, which still smells new.

She opens the book, carefully lifting the pages from the right hand corner and guiding them to the left, dropping them, in a gentle heap, when she lifts her hand for the next lot of pages till she finds the one that she needs. And, she looks out of the window again.

*   *   *

A pigeon tugs with its beak at a loose wire dangling against a water pipe, flapping its wings in vexed frustration at the wire that will not come loose.

– stupidest bird on the planet. The only reason it is not extinct is because they feed it in Bombay – the souls of saints and all that. The constant easy feeding has made it lazy and dumb...Bombay's own Dodo. The Lucky Dodo. Will only multiply competing with the human population of this city. No extinction.

A crow finds the eggs they lay randomly and these fat birds, consumed by lethargy, cannot find the energy to grieve.

This exercise with the wires is the only real movement you ever seen from them, all effort wasted on a wire, which will not come loose, when there is a mountain of nest-building materials available in this city. He will report to his wife that he could not find anything. He'll ask her to carry on, lay the eggs wherever she thinks fit.

She will find a stray flower-pot in a random window-grill because there are no balconies in Bombay. Or the pigeon will lay it on the top of a cupboard near the window of a cluttered house where the old Grandfather, in a white vest, not shy of his wasted muscles, will chuck it out of the window because he no longer fears the wrath of the Gods for this act of violence.

he is with her when she lays them,

nodding, bobbing, curtsying his head in the *Prakampita Greevabheda that I learnt in Bharatnatayam class...*

gurgling, nodding, bobbing, curtsying...while the female lays their eggs...

Pigeons are vermin. –

* * *

– why doesn't my hand stay on these pages? Why don't my eyes read the words?

Why am I so tired, so bored with this? My profession? My work? Work was worship.

I have lost faith... –

She stares out of her window at the deep blue of the sea crowded with port-borne vessels, at small, short waves that hit the embankment and bounce away to collide into others like themselves reflecting a sparkling November sun.

– what day is it?

They are right about my notice board. I really ought to tidy up. Layers and layers of notes and stuff. Where the hell is the calendar?

Twenty-sixth of November Two Thousand and Eight.

Not an important date. Just another day. It will end soon. I will not know that time has passed me by. I will dream and sleep and wake up tomorrow and today will repeat itself tomorrow and the day after.

I am twenty-seven years old and nine months and some days...on this day, the 26th of November 2008...I like to think of the date like this, in this format.

I don't like those permutations of the 'mm/dd/yy' and the 'dd/mm/yy' formats...it has to be a combination of numerical and words...balanced...language with mathematics, yin and yang, poetry and calculation, truism and a theorem.

Just numbers makes it impersonal...26/11/2008...and just words makes it... makes it...too long? –

*   *   *

Meera yawns.
A yellow post-it note gets her attention. It reads, 'MAKING A SACRIFICE'.

– forgot about that! –

It had been put up there so that she would look up from her work, to find it there. It would remind her to think of something. A reminder.

She had pinned it there, when?

Fifteen days ago? A month and fifteen days ago?

She is awake now.

– I forgot to look at it! I don't believe this! –

Suddenly energized, she minimizes the open pages of her DELL notebook to access her 'Favourites' folder.

– which one was it? Which one was it? The Three Penny Review? Some cute name like that…The Little…no? It wasn't an Indian mag. Writers' Guild? I think so!

Oh God! Please don't say I have missed the deadline! – She hasn't. The website, very witty, proclaims that she still has some more days to make her submission. Five thousand words. Times New Roman, Font 12. Theme, 'Making a Sacrifice'.

She dials, 'AJ' on her mobile.

we are watching 'Alexander'
he says, 'You are my Hephaestion…'
'And you are mine. I cannot believe you just pronounced his name!'

Higher love.

He had called her suddenly and out of the blue last night. After months. She expects him not to answer but then he does.

"Hi, AJ! Are you at work? Can we speak?"

"Wassup, Meera! Of course we can speak."

"You remember 'Making a Sacrifice'?"

"Yes. Have you come up with something?"

"No. I haven't. I mean, I forgot about it! Completely. Can you believe that?"

"Yes, I can believe that."

"Oh! Please! I do have a theme though, now that it is all coming back to me! I *had* thought about it. Do you have the time?"

"For you, I always have the time, Alexander."

"You haven't had the time for me for months! And I am Hephaestion because you were A."

"Whichever. We caught up last night! Come on. Tell me about your theme."

Was that condescension she heard?

"Right. My theme. Don't yawn over the phone though, okay? Don't let me know if it is killing you, okay?"

"I won't."

"It's like this...and this is just thinking out loud, right...making a sacrifice is something you do with each decision that you make, with each path that you choose, you let go of the other, or others...*that* is the sacrifice. The fact that you will never know how things might have turned out, had you taken the other paths...where you would have turned up, had you chosen Option A instead of Option B. Are you there?"

"Yes."

"Okay. So I set the story somewhere in the desert. The Thar Desert in Pakistan. And there is a family with too many to feed and some sons to spare. You know? Word spreads that someone is recruiting, the money is good, and glory imminent. His parents think it a good idea that he provide for the family. The condition is that he doesn't maintain any contact with the world that he will have to leave behind. He hears the first few sermons and is convinced that this is the direction his life must take. Not necessarily for the glory that they promise but when he hears of...and...he hears from...the other boys who belong here about how comfortable their families are and all that. So he gives up his world to move on into his version of a job, which is a sacrifice. His family gives him up, without too much ado. It is all very practical and matter of fact, with the added benefit of being for the greater good. That is a sacrifice. He is taught and learns a violent, intolerant interpretation of his Holy Text, which is sacrificing the peace and the good that he could have learnt about. He trains to be a warrior of sorts, which is when he sacrifices the gully cricket that he played with his friends. His teachers are making the same or similar sacrifices. They work hard to instill hate. They give up on love? Do you think they give up on love? Maybe not. They *love* their God, so in a way, they give up on loving his *creation.* They give up on a *type* of love."

She stops to think. A moment of inspiration is not enough to fuel a monologue, much less a five-thousand word story.

She fumbles. "It goes on like that, hmmm? What do you think? It doesn't have to be a fantastic setting, it could be us. Anything. Each decision we make, is a sacrifice. And we don't even know it. You with me?"

"It will be great. You will narrate it well."

"The theme must reflect in the story. It should be evident without being *stated.* That is the tough part. I cannot talk down to the reader."

"Good. So, send me a draft! Set a target and finish the story."

"It is hackneyed, isn't it? I mean, it is the story of a terrorist, and may even take a sympathetic view of the fellow and how he too *lost* something. Usual stuff. Done umpteen times. Also, peculiar to the Indian situation, local porn, unimaginative. Very origins of 9/11 kind of crap."

"Come on, Mee! Most stories are usual. You just write them differently – Wilde and Wodehouse had the same issues."

"I won't write differently. It will be the same description desperately seeking to prove that a desolate desert and accompanying poverty is beautiful, that the fellow actually misses his 'home', when what he had was really an apology of a shack and parents who did it without thinking and then regretted the number that they came up with because there were that many mouths to feed… some description of fauna, which my hero would not notice while he was home but which will come back to him on a lonely night before all hell breaks loose in some country or the other but the memory will not be enough to make him turn away. The story is a ploy by a loser author to ask the world for sympathy for a man who deserves a royal slaughtering, at best."

"'Writers' block again? Or do you just want to turn into the literary critic that you are?"

"Not again. It continues on and on and on. It is perpetual. I am not a writer, never was. There is not a thought in my head that someone has not already covered. And I am talking only about the English language here. Everything's already been thought of. This is the end of innovation. It's everywhere. We don't celebrate breakthroughs in technology or science, we read nonchalantly about the Nobel Prize for this or that. Because somebody already dreamed up what was to come. The guy who actually achieved it outside of the novel or movie does not surprise us anymore. He must make do with adulation in a limited circle capable of appreciating his work even when what he has done affects so many more of us. And we say, 'Oh that? I thought we'd already done it, no? It was in the *Minority Report*, or *Star Wars* or the *Time Machine* or something…' I don't think I'll do it, AJ. It will never win. It will be like one of Gogh's studies."

"Why should it have to win? You don't have to even send it for the competition. Just write for yourself!"

"What are you, man? Why would I write for me? I don't want to be famous after I'm *dead*. I would write for the world besides, I am done with noble notions, AJ. So childish. Gogh went mad trying to sell his stuff and killed himself for his failure. Acceptance pal, acknowledgement! That feeds the artist. Face it."

AJ's laughing at the outburst, "Okay! Now you're talking! I never thought you wanted to write to get published, Mee! If that is the case, you'd better get down to completing the projects you have started on."

– the *'projects you have started on'*?

Where are the projects I have started on?

How does he know this? How much does he know? Have I discussed *everything* with him? I don't remember! I don't remember! –

Meera is less animated now. "It's no use. They'll never be published. Definitely not by these literary mags. They publish psycho stuff, I can't read a minute of it without dying… actually, no… grapes are sour… there is some good stuff there. I mean, yes. Whatever."

"Simplicity in presentation gets published! Except, when Rushdie writes…"

"But seriously, they are not looking at our kind of writing. I wish that we had studied literature and writing styles and all."

"What? And killed the romance? You would have hated literature had you studied it. You would have wanted to become a lawyer. I do see your point about the end of innovation, though. That is why I keep going back to the Renaissance - so many greats, all together and then, really, nothing."

"Okay. Brilliant. So those are your real thoughts. Encouraging. I'll just go chop off my ear now. Which one was it? The left, I think."

"No! Don't do it just yet. Send me a study that I can constructively criticize for you, which would then inspire you more properly to do what you have to do…"

"Right. Ha ha. Listen, I have to go now. There is this response to a query that I have been drafting for the past two hours and all."

"Sure! Call me when you need a sounding board."

Their giggling goodbye still leaves her unnerved.

– why do we do this? This thing…play games, make plans…like you did when you were kids? War games.

Speaking about it like you knew what you were talking about…dead serious…and discussing *projects* that I am *working* on?

Like what? Like I was going to complete any of that stuff? Like I even remembered that this is what I wanted to really, really, really do?

Can you surprise yourself every day? How can you forget the projects you have started on?

How can you remain perpetually distracted from ambition? So distracted that you forget the ambition?

How can you wake up in the morning and not remember what you did the previous day? The promises you made. To yourself?

How can you forget your purpose, act like you had none?

And live off the clues that you left for yourself?

Like Hansel. Breadcrumbs on Post-It notes…and you don't even *know* that you are lost…at least Hansel and Gretel *knew* they were lost…   −

Shiny black shoes, white shirt, grey skirt, maroon tie and belt - my school uniform
I am clutching at a chit. It reads: A Hot Day
I am dying.
the other kids all got topics that we had prepared for…
festivals, moral science, civic sense, the environment …
I am not prepared for this…A Hot Day?
not using my three minutes! my mind is blank…yes, it can go blank because it has…
a picnic? shall I run away? what about a hot day? shall I faint?
better than continuing to look a fool...
they just called my name…my turn!
why am I walking towards the dais?
what confidence I must exude! what a joke I will be in the next few seconds!

one of them, he doesn't teach my class, is nodding encouragingly at me...
but it is too late...I mumble something about a picnic on a very hot day...
all the tips forgotten, all the general beginnings that we had prepared...
four wives and a husband - who, why, when, what and how...
prolonged silence...is my time not up yet?
the kids start to fidget...the organisers exchange glances
  — How to put an end to her pain...? —
'I'm sorry.' I say
walking out a moment before they come to get me...
the pitiable walk of the beaten...

Her cursor hits the 'Personal' folder where she finds her 'writing'. She finds four files variously named, 'Delirium', 'Thought 1', and 'A Marriage Less Perfect'.

– I wrote the stuff in these files! And he knows about it...he knows and remembers. How could *I* forget?

No! How could I forget? –

Her hands are clammy.

– why do hands get *clammy*?

Are there even supposed to be sweat glands there? Or is it some other fluid...that surfaces only when your mouth is dry... –

I am walking with Mum around the football field in the

Armed Forces Medical College campus

I am wishing for something that I really want…what was it?

I am looking up at the sky for the evening star of superstition…

my heart jumps when I find it gleaming brightly at me

…first star I see tonight…

and I make that wish…

Mum's walking on the track far opposite me…

beyond her, in the horizon, beyond the goal-post of the football field, I see

a bright star…another bright star

I turn around to the one that I had wished upon…it is not as bright.

The cosmos conspired to cheat me.

my wish will not come true

I defiantly retort, 'I will get what I want. I must work for it, right? I will.'

I don't wish upon evening stars again

no wishes to be made, none to be granted…

what did I want that evening? was it a grade? was I ill prepared for an exam?

did it come true…? my wish…?

star light…star bright…

I wish I may…wish I might…have the wish I wish tonight…

– what had I wished for? I cannot remember. –

The rude ringing of the desk phone, breaks her daydream.

"Are you coming down to the conference room?"

"For what...?"

"The meeting, sweetheart! Look at your calendar! Didn't you get the invite? Do you dismiss your reminders or something? They are all waiting for you! Come quickly. Quickly!"

– something *had* popped up...and why the hell is the receptionist sounding so frustrated, and condescending? She wants to be me, does she? Uneducated bimbo...–

She had not 'dismissed' it, had she?

– no. I hadn't 'dismissed' it. –

It was 'snoozing'.

It would have popped up again and she would have run for the meeting. She still had a minute.
She did not like the cheekiness of the secretarial staff in assuming her dismissal of the Firm's tasks, even if they were as mundane as they were.

She stands up to see empty cubicles, their occupants all gone.

– when did they all disappear? –

She trudges down the stairs. No time to wait for the elevator.

She cannot respond to the receptionist's warm smile, her wounds still fresh from the recent presumptuous tease about the 'dismissal' of tasks.

– why are they even having this meeting?

Something about billing and other affairs. Like that can matter to me today!

Shall I just tell them, *'I'm not really late. Just didn't plan on staying for this one. Hope that's alright?'*

But that wouldn't be cricket… *'when you've promised a thing, you're bound to do it'*… *'if I turned around, I would certainly rue it'*… 'Rue it'… would… should? *Should* certainly rue it?

Davis? Some Davis. The first poem in the Class 9 poetry textbook… how I loved that poem. *The Sportsman…*

The road was hilly, the wind was strong,
The laddie gallantly struggled or something along
With never a glance at the downward way…

Was it?

Where his mates or friends something and laughed in play
If I turned around… blah blah
Bound to do it…

Bound. Tied. Stuck.

Inspiring poem. It had made me try so hard.

I don't like being late but I usually am.

Maybe I like being late.
Infinitely does the minute last! Upto the sixtieth second and then, without knowing when and how, you're late... –

She crawls into the last chair in the board room realizing that they notice her without breaking the continuity of their discussions.
– which is good...nobody really waits, do they? The receptionist told me that they were *waiting* for me.

They must've called the receptionist and asked her to check on me because they were *waiting* for me. But that is not so.

No one waits for you.

Everyone is the time and the tide.

Are you ever important enough to anyone?

And should it be your life's goal to be that one person they do wait for?

How long would you like them to wait for you?
Not forever! That would make legend, myth, or religion.

It isn't the same as immortality.

Immortality: will people remember you after you are dead?

My question is a little more important than that of immortality. It is a question of your significance among people who you know, people who know you.

And it is a question that you will have the answers to, while you live, irrespective of whether you ask the question or not.

The question that I am asking is not pertinent in some parts of Africa or a remote village in India where people are usually more hungry than important.

They would repeatedly ask themselves about food, I guess.

Their philosophers would use metaphors of hunger and feasting and war.

Does that make my concerns pale with superfluity?

Or do I comfort myself with the belief that we were all born to a destiny?

It is not my destiny, in this life, to worry too much about food…at least not on the same scale as the people in some parts of Africa and that village in India.

It is my mandate to wonder about the perils of being forgotten *before* I am dead … about comprising matter that doesn't matter…–

The slide-show has progressed to a chart of billability, money notionally and actually earned, recoveries made and pending. Her team features in the higher rungs of this list. She is embarrassed.

– how long will this last? This transient glory… –

Does she continue to worry about losing it? Is *it* what she wanted? Glory among the nine or ten people seated in this room? Her massive belly is assurance that it will pass.

– things slow down, priorities change and one day, they forget to call you.

The meeting carries on and it doesn't matter that the preset reminder on your digital calendar is the only thing urging you to be present.

Ten people from among the hundred that you work with could forget you.

Ten out of the thousand people you know could forget.

A thousand out of the millions who you don't know could stop inviting you to join their Orkut network.

Your family will take a little longer to stop asking about you but they do not count. They are obliged to remember - you are born to that privilege as a grandchild, a nephew, a son, a daughter. And even then, you could lose it all.

Some shun this materialism.

Social ascetics. People who neither succumb to nor harbour any notions of their worth or anybody else's. They skip along stopping to smell the daisies on the way. They don't care to check whether those that they had started out with were waiting for them, or whether they would continue – once done with the daisies – in the company of the same people. They may not even worry about walking alone.

It is possible to be a social ascetic about anything.

In fact, it is ironical because this sort of Social Asceticism may just be your insurance against the forgetfulness that you fear. It could mean immortality. But it takes courage because you could variously be the nerd, the maverick, the saint, the freak, the outcast, even the outlaw!

Or. Or you could be the writer – a poet who brings common language, everyday words, together to make a lyric, a song that can be sung. –

She sits behind her open notebook, ostensibly taking notes now and then, until her writing becomes more furious and she writes, 'Making a Sacrifice' on the top of a blank page, underlining it twice and then thrice, a bolder, less rickety straighter, third.

– the notebook and my pencil...subterfuge and camouflage...they don't know what I am doing! An adventure...! –

She writes:

He devoured the tandoori chicken within minutes.

'Half portion?' the waiter had asked, accommodating this customer who sat alone.

'Full' he had said dismissing the kind gesture.

He worked his way through it like the man that he was, losing himself in the delicious juices of well cooked chicken that had been marinated long enough for the masala to be absorbed by the layers of white meat beneath the reddish-brown crust of the first few membranes.

His hands worked while his mouth chewed, and morsel followed bite. He did not stop when some of the oil trickled down the end of a half-eaten leg, running down the palm of his hand, past the valley of the Mounts of Venus and the Moon *and along the Lines of Life and Fate, onto his wrist soaking into the cuffs of his white shirt. The developing stain would not come off even if he tried now. He decides that the shirt was due for dry cleaning in any case. (<u>CHK: is it 'mound' or mount?</u>)*

He had not stopped to wonder if he was really hungry. He could not stop to consider if he was full.

Gone was the pledge of moderation that the overweight fellow had made. Once more, the door to excess was open. Once more, just once more let promises be sacrificed to the tantalizing taste of indulgence. He ate as if he would, his last meal.

He was never really done. He continued to gnaw at the soft cartilage and then chewed into the bone, pitying himself and the genus chicken for the lack of marrow in its bones.

He wondered now if he should have asked for the lamb instead… –

They are looking at her. They expect her to say something.

Someone says something about 'WIP' and status.

– what the hell is W-I-P? –
"Sorry!" she grins. "I think that I missed some of that. What is W-I-P?"

"Work in Progress," they say in unison.

"Yes. Sure. Well there is really just one transaction for now and a couple of opinions…"

They smile. "No…this is about the outstanding bills for the month, honey."

"Right. Ah…can I get back to you?"

They understand. No rush. Someone is going to bring the list to her. The secretaries will help her with the draft bills.

With that the meeting is almost done but the Senior Associates will stay back with the Mentoring Partner. He is going to take up the piece on pending recoveries for previous months.

She balks.

– it has been forty-five minutes already!
I'm ravenous.

This is bloody pop-quiz treatment…I have to get out.

I have to leave. Move on.

Precious time. –

"Who wants to go first? I have your accounts here with me," he says thoughtfully laying out the spreadsheets in front of him. "I invite you to appear in any order that you choose! As you see, I am ready."

They see the sadistic glint in his eye past the green hue of his anti-reflection glasses. It will be past lunch time before he is done.

"Can I go first, if that's alright?"

"Sure!"

The others are almost grateful that it isn't them already.

He picks her list out with his elegantly long fingers, the purposeful élan of one who watches himself perform each action, say each word, complete each sentence and accompany all of this with an appropriate, perhaps practiced, expression.

he steps out of himself to look at himself
he leans against the boardroom wall, hands in pockets, one shoulder against the wall, staring at himself with a critical air, which is a mask for the wonder he feels because he is God's gift to mankind.
Each of him is conscious of the other.
One of him sits interacting with the mortals while the other stands and
may even circle the room but
they cannot take their eyes off each other, they are both in awe of him.

– no one likes him…he believes that this means he's doing his 'job'. He's a prick.

Why call him 'Mentoring' partner? Why not 'Overseeing'? Or 'Supervising'? Or 'Policing'?

A lawyer understands the emphasis on the appropriate words and phrases. A lawyer works on them as hard as the poet.

'A poet could not be but gay,
In such a jocund company'

What if Longfellow had said something else?

Was it not Wordsworth? The Daffodils?

No. Longfellow.

'a poet could not be but glad
For joy that dancing Daffodils had…'

But then he'd have nothing rhyming with 'glee'…'*Out-did the sparkling waves in glee'*.

'a poet would have to be
Happy in such company!'

That would have made 'be' and 'company'. Would it have broken his rhythm or the lyrical scheme, had both rhymed with 'glee'?

Wouldn't 'Blithe' have worked? But he uses 'jocund' right there in the middle of it all.
It stands out, like a scab on smooth daffodil-skin.

*'Night's candles are burnt out, and jocund day
Stands tip-toe on the misty mountain tops...'*

Why not, *'happy* day' standing tip-top on misty mountain tops? Why *'jocund'*?

A word used only by poets. –

"You are really back of the class. Almost last, maybe even last," he says smirking at his summary of her statement, clicking his tongue and shaking his head with disapproving disappointment.

He taps his pencil on the laminated veneer table top not looking at her at all, looking instead at each of them one-by-one, a slight nodding of his head, as if he were listening to a quick beat that only the both of *him* could hear.

This is her cue.

"I'm going to clear it all up... soon."

"Now?"

"Not now, I'm sorry. I'm going to have to quit for now but it will be done tomorrow. Promise!"

"You do realize that this has been pending for rather long now, don't you? I had sent you a mail last week."

"You had?"

"Yes! And I received no response."

"Must've missed it, obviously… I mean, it has been busy and all."

"Fine. Go. But I will remember that you promised!"

"Sure! In fact, you won't have to remember at all! Thanks!" she says, grabbing her notebook and heading out.

– such relief!

She walks to the door and out,
Happy steps, jocund mood, a silent shout!
Jocund! Jocund! Jocund!

Yes! It is a word used only by poets! –

*   *   *

She'll return to her desk, grab her bags and get out. It is well past noon. Responses to e-mails, challenges, snags, glitches, everything, will wait.

She hurriedly drafts a holding response to the delisting query that had been impossible to concentrate on this morning. But, the yellow post-it, 'MAKING A SACRIFICE', is impossible to ignore. She sits down.

– who are the people that make a sacrifice?

What can I use as a subject? Think. Think.

Why must it be usual people?

To begin with, it will be usual people! How can I possibly arrive at a theme the day that I am born? Why the debilitating hurry to be original and different? Why not usual people, unusually written?

Oh yes! Do that. Write it unusually. Let me help you, usual would be mothers.

Mothers? Yes. Mothers. Of course! I wrote a paper for my Women's Studies course. I had called it, 'Motherhood, the Defined and Constraining Norm'.

A usual subject for Women's Studies, I'm sure.

So what?

No, nothing. Carry on…write about a mother, making a sacrifice…–

The voices in her head wait in respectful silence. She stares at the blinking cursor on a new document. She will type this time.

He walks away with you…
As if you were his…

At different times in your life
You will carry something
A horseshoe, a silver coin, a pagan-looking charm a sweet boy
gave you,
You will carry them believing that they protect you
I will be these charms for you…

Leave me here
So that for now, your world is not ugly…

He is waiting for her to finish what she is doing. She must do it smoothly, minimize the window, because it does not look like a legal document.

Alt and Tab.

Back on the credulous Outlook.

She turns to him. "Hi!"

"I wanted to show you some pictures."

"Of?"

"My trek."

She has to be interested, hasn't she? She cannot be dismissive, and rude, can she? She smiles, "Let's see them!"

He moves to her desk, accessing her computer to log on to his blog. "I think you will like these. There is more green between Dhakuri to Loharkhet and you like green hills more than snow-covered ones, don't you."

"Where did you trek up to?"

"Oh! I went right up to the Pindar Glacier but I haven't uploaded those yet."

– slide show.
Mountains.

Sky. Clear days.

No clouds.

Grass.

Hill flora.

Smiling faces.

Too happy.
Smoking tea in their hands.

Natives. Also happy.

Wait….! –

"Stop. What was that? Can we go back? How do you stop the slide show?"

He stops the show taking her back to the preceding photographs. "I thought that the slide show would be better because it moves faster. I know that you were leaving…"

"No. Yes. That's fine. Stop here. Is that a grave?"
"Yes."

"In the middle of the path you were trekking?"

"Yes. I mean, it is on the mountain path, yes. Not in the middle though. It is at a convenient place on the side."

"No graveyards around?"

"Now that you mention it, no. No graveyards around."

"Whose is it?"

"Peter Kost. Shall I zoom in for you to read the… what is it called?"

"Epitaph."

"Here. Now you can read it."

– '10.08.1944 + 03.06.2000'.

'YOUR PARADISE IS HERE'. –

"He was fifty-five," she observes, "and ten months, some days."

"Yes. They told us about it when we started out at Dhakuri. The tea stall guy's dad was there when he died of a heart-attack on this trail, very close to where he is buried."

"Was he on his way to the glacier? Or was he on his way back?"
"Oh, his party was on their way back."

"Hmmm. Were his family with him? Who wrote the epitaph? Who gave them permission to bury him right there? Overlooking the mountains? Who allowed them to put a tombstone there? Is it very expensive to take a body back? But I suppose the middle of the mountains is many days distance from an airport."

"I don't know."

"He was German?"

"I think so."

"How was his paradise *here*? He probably loved the Alps more than the Himalayas, no? Or did he love the mountains generally? I'm a beach-person, myself."

He is laughing. "I never really thought of all this!"

"No?" She looks at him. "Can I look at this some more? Let's look at the others another time?"
"Of course! I am glad that you are interested! See you tomorrow!"

She frowns at the picture of the grave.

Embarrassing tears that must be wiped away quickly.

Thank God that the others aren't yet back from that sick meeting.

The overwhelming sadness weighs her down and she does not move. Then, a mad impatience takes over.

– I have to find your face! Where will I find you? On Orkut?

What a way for us to meet! I live, Peter Kost, and you are dead. They know you though along the path from Dhakuri village to Loharkhet. They don't know me.

You were Christian. They buried you.

We don't bury our dead, we burn them. Like they burnt Eric Bana, no, Hector in *Troy*, minus the gold coins over the eyes.
In fact, these days it is electrical. No smoke, no odor, no bones to pick from among the ashes, no skull to crack so

that the brain burns with the rest of your organs and you don't carry memories of this life to the next.

Most hygienic.

I won't find you on Orkut. You can hardly have registered at your age? Not if you were the type that trekked mountains and died while doing that. You probably met enough people on your journeys.

Maybe your children put you on a blog or something? With pictures. It would make a fine story – the father they lost to the Himalayas.

Were you happy, when you collapsed, I mean, satisfied?

Is there such a thing as a last thought?

I have Jewish friends. Did you resent what the world did to Germany, post-Hitler? Talk about it at Christmas dinners when the conversation swung towards politics?

Were you embarrassed about Hitler's Germany?
On the stones near your grave invisible people with invisible hands have painted the words, 'Om Mani Padme Hum'.

I know those words.

They gifted me a stone with these words once when I was at a Basecamp store.
The salesgirl was not clear when I asked her what it meant. She said it was for luck. The trekkers at the store

told me that these words were almost an internationally accepted trekkers' code for 'a happy and successful journey'.

I like it that these stones are close to your grave. Your journey was successful and I want to believe, happy.

But *Om Mani Padme Hum* is a six syllable mantra in Tibetan Buddhism. It invokes the protector from danger. You don't need that now, do you?

Did you know the Dalai Lama or of him, Peter Kost?

With their colourful flags peculiar to Tibetan settlements and their maroon robes and *momos* – that succulent food now also available in the malls of Bombay – the Himalayas belong to them, or to anyone who lives in the tiresome tedious beauty of those mountains.

Did you believe that there were things worth dying for? Worth *living* for?

Who called for the priest? There must be Christian priests even in those parts. They still carry the White Man's burden even though they are quite brown and their English, terribly accented. Did he say the right prayers for you? You have sects in Christianity too, don't you?

More people know you now than did when you lived, I am sure. They stop at your grave and learn about your death, your name. You cannot pass by a spot like that without staring at the peaks that surround your grave, without coming closer to the ledge of that hill, to look at the valley that cradles you.

Like the Sufi Saints of the Muslims, you lie closer, in death, to God, to Heaven, or Paradise, or whatever. Your grave is a shrine. You lie where you can see, hear and help the living.

Or can you, Peter Kost?

If I died now, just now on this day, the 26th of November 2008, would they bury me here? Near my desk, a little to the side, not in anyone's way? Would *my* epitaph be, 'YOUR PARADISE IS HERE'?

Or would they find that post-it and make it my epitaph?

'MAKING A SACRIFICE'?

And would they find the little that I wrote and publish it somewhere? *The projects that I was working on…*

If I died here, just now, what would my last thought be?

But you will not die here! What a silly thought!

How would *you* know that, Peter Kost?

Did you think that you would breathe your last between Loharkhet and Dhakuri villages? What would you know? –

With feverish frenzy now, she slams her laptop shut and leaves for the day not bothering with goodbyes.

12:45 P.M.

She moves closer to the mirrored back wall of the elevator examining her dark circles wondering why they remained in spite of the fairly decent sleep she was supposed to be getting, and all those supplements she was on.

– but it is not a decent sleep…it's nightmarish, damn it…*iron* deficiency, maybe?

I am out. In the open.

Bright afternoon. *Not* a hot day. Make some Vitamin D. Just right. –

'it was stage fright…nothing to worry about, just thought I'd let you know that it did not go too well…I hope you will go easy on her…it wasn't an assessment or anything, she is so confident otherwise…yes…I think it was a terrible topic, you know…? 'A Picnic' or something, or 'A Hot Day'…The other speakers got topics that were so much better…'

– that is probably how she spoke. I am sure one of the teachers had called them to warn them about my pitiable defeat at the Extempore Competition. –

I am home.

Dad's standing at the door. He nods happily at me, 'Ice cream!'

They are all in the dining room

Like there is a party on or something

Ice cream… And cake.

'I could not speak…struck dumb…' I confess even though they didn't ask me about it.

'That's alright…happens to all great speakers…no one is not nervous, you know that…'

'I looked an ass…'

'the audience admires anyone who has the guts to go up there…you don't win them all…'

'I just stood there…You don't lose the way I did, either…not like this…'

'What was your topic?'

'A Hot Day'

'What? A Hot Day? That is silly…you were struck dumb by how silly it was…'

'It was simple, too simple for a three-minute-extempore competition.

Next time we will work on the simple and silly possibilities as much as the tough, meaningful ones...be prepared for anything...'

Voices...all sorry for me...I am sorry for me...I eat cake and ice cream.

*   *   *

We walk that evening. Dad says, 'We don't always need a complex thought to build meaning into it...part of the challenge in telling a story is how meaningful you can make the mundane...'

'How do you add meaning to, 'A Hot Day'?'

'Now, this is not fair because I have had most of the evening to think about it and you had just three minutes...but only as an example, let's do something with 'A Hot Day'!

Do you remember the suicides over the reservations-for-scheduled-castes issue?

The Mandal Commission and how it demanded job reservations for certain classes of people based on caste, the ensuing instances of self-immolation by students who revolted against this policy?'

'Yes...I remember...it was last year... the pictures from the papers are still in my head...'

'Good...now...imagine this,

it was a cool night, as some of Delhi's nights between September and October are...and I was walking down a road...I was suddenly disturbed by some loud shouting in the distance...I walked briskly towards the sound.

The voice was a slogan...many slogans...they had a rhythm to them. I wanted to hear what they were saying...like a chant...a chant that always climaxed in a shout...

There was a funny, familiar smell in the air that night.

In the middle of that huge circle, a young man was leading the slogans...

then he took a can of kerosene and poured it all over himself...he lit a match, dropping it ceremoniously at his feet...

that was it! The funny, familiar smell...was kerosene oil...

he was alight that exact second...the slogans became muddled shouts and screams...

girls screamed...the circle split...in frenzy...someone threw a blanket on the lit man...

he threw it off himself...he wanted to burn...

I couldn't stay to watch anymore...I am a child, I thought, these people are all in college...grown up...

I started to run away...but I could feel the heat of the flames and I could hear the screaming for a long time afterwards...I could smell flesh and hair burning...

I still can.

Can you imagine what a hot, bright day feels like on a cool Delhi night?'

– is that what I am doing today? Finding meaning in the mundane…? –

She reaches for her phone, "Hullo. Mummy?"
"Hi, sweetheart! How are you? So, are you calling a friend over tonight? Will you manage alone?"

"No…I will manage…I want to manage alone, need some time to myself…I watched a pretty nasty flick last night, you know…I am taking the time to think. I am trying to make the mundane more…"

"Should I call you back, Meera? Nothing urgent, *na*? We are hosting some friends for lunch. Bye!"

– just like that…she hangs up on me.

How did she presume that I'd take her call when she called me back? Once she was done hosting friends for lunch.

She should want to listen to me! About *Savior*, about stuff that she should know about me…the way I look, how much I weigh, what I'm wearing, how I've been, and why I want to be alone…!

Why *do* I want to be alone? Why did I call her?

We speak about things in the future…a call that will be made…a call that she expects will be answered.

What if I didn't answer? How would you like that?

What if I don't answer at all?

Ever? –

*   *   *

She walks towards a group of huddled collegians waiting for the bus. She doesn't smile at the sound of their unselfconsciously loud youthful voices.

They crowd around a pleasantly surprising sight, a dash of green, leafy branch darting out of nowhere from behind a boundary wall to one of those ugly buildings, topped with a bright purple-wine-pink flower breathing amidst the surrounding rot.

"It *is* a Hibiscus!"

"No. It cannot be. It looks like something different. Where is that thing that peeps out of a Shoe-flower?"

"Stigma! Stamen?"
"Different type of Hibiscus *hai, yaar!*"

Her heart beats faster. How shall she get their attention? Should she put a hand on one of their lean shoulders? Would that be proper? She is older, she can take that liberty, no? What if they push it away? Ask her what the hell she wants? What if they think her a cougar, or something?

But she needn't worry because they make way for her, as they would want the young to make way for them when they are about her age. And she, in gracious acknowledgement of their common pasts and futures, smiles at their good manners and says to them, as she walks blithely by, "It's an Allamanda, not a Hibiscus."

She keeps it fleeting, their interaction - the interlude between two phases of youth, not so apart as to be differing generations. She glances at them when she says what she has wanted to say since the time that she could hear their languidly laughing argument. To show them that what they were arguing about could be important to the way that they will turn out.

She looks away when she is assured of their smiling thanks, and wonder, and hope, and all the effect that she had wanted to have on their thoughts, if only for that moment.

*   *   *

– they think I am a rock-star. That I know my work, my clearly corporate, grey, black and white work, and that I also know that purple-wine-pink flower, *Allamanda*.

They think I must be interesting, successful, and interesting, like the sound of the flower, *Allamanda*.

They think that I am what they want to be. Like this flower, rare and beautiful. The best of the best. Not common. Not a Hibiscus.

They think that I must know more. They see that I have something to teach them. The names of many flowers maybe?

What a sense of mystery surrounds me as they watch me walk away! They may not discuss it but their eyes will say what they are thinking. And what they are thinking requires a closeted atmosphere for voicing, even to oneself. Not that bus stop, even with the *Allamanda* smiling, watching beautifully over them…what they are feeling, the plans they make for success requires just a close friend or two and some really sentimental crap aided maybe by a couple of pegs of the right kind of alcohol…it will start with a discussion of how they would buy Black Label instead of the Imperial Blue quarter that they can barely manage to save pocket-money for…

I have created frauds.

One of them at least will remember that flower and the effect that its name had on them all, the clarification delivered with superior grace, beautiful fleeting condescension that would be wasted if it weren't mimicked at first opportunity.

One day, he will use that name to surprise his listeners...*Allamanda*.

And that is all he will know about beauty, in addition to the Hibiscus.

Just like me.

I do that with grammar sometimes. –

*   *   *

they joke about my being constantly late
I retort, 'Ah! The use of the past-continuous tense expressing irritation! But misplaced irritation because the facts are incorrect. There is hope however, for the grammar, at least!'
we laugh the adverse laughter of colleagues...

– I use my knowledge of the rules of grammar to make a joke out of a joke.

I confuse them with this deflection to the rules of grammar in my retort. I look smarter. Superior.

The kind of person who makes no mistakes. You should know how you speak in front of me because...ooh! She knows her grammar!
But that's not true. I am a fraud. It sounds complicated, the *past-continuous* tense, to those who have forgotten their lessons. But it is really simple. And I never understood grammar...I just use the little that I know to live the fib that I have been living...there it is again. The past-continuous...tense. –

a birthday party. We are playing Pin-the-Donkey's-Tail…

The other games have been played and won…I won nothing…

Uncle keeps warning us, 'No cheating!'

because we are making our ambitions and our methods so obvious…

It is my turn…he ties the black band around my eyes so tight,

quashing the vitreous humour out of my eyeballs and I can see nothing…nothing at all!

black blankness and that red, dark-red blackness

the blood and tissue of my closed eyelids pushing against my corneas…

And I say, 'I can see…there is a slit…'

My voice is small but he hears me, 'Can you? Let me tie it again…'

Why did I say that?

He would tie it tighter…I would not win…

'Maybe Uncle, if you loosened it a little the folds wouldn't stretch so much…'

Is there really any logic to that?

'Here…can you see now?'

'No…it is alright now…'

*   *   *

– what if he had checked to confirm if I could really see?

What if he had mimed boxing at me to see if I dodged or reacted to his fist aimed at my head?

I wouldn't have moved because I could not see a thing to save my life...

What if they had caught me pathetically trying, only trying, to cheat? –

>   *I miss the Donkey's bum by a mile...*
>   *Everyone laughs the laugh that I have been laughing when the others missed...*
>   *the laugh of the hopeful...the laugh of losers...not so different...*

>   *They are announcing the prizes...I should have pinned closer to the Donkey's bum to win...*

>   *'The last game is special! We will move to the dining room after this to cut the cake! (happy cheering!)*
>   *And the prizes have to be special too!*
>   *One is for the winner... somebody always wins...'*

>   *We clap...I can feel the tears coming and I don't want to stop them...*
>   *Then he says, 'But there are other winners...people who will win in Life...so this really, really, really special prize is for the courageous girl,*
>   *who did not cheat, even though she had the chance...'*
>   *Yes.*
>   *Me!*
>   *A bar of chocolate wrapped in shiny pink paper...*

silver, gold stars on the shiny pink paper...my prize!'

*   *   *

– I hate lies...and liars...and everything that makes you want to lie, *have* to lie...

I am walking too slowly. It is so crowded. Is it like this at this time every day? Will it get more crowded than this? I wonder if they are done with that meeting at office. They must've ordered a working lunch or something.

I should have said something else to the 'Mentoring-bloody-Partner' when he said that I was back of the class...
I should've said, *'Back of the class? Are you kidding? I am so happy just to be in this class!'*

That would've been a good 'FO'! They would've all smiled... hidden smiles...

But not at the joke that I made...
no, they aren't smiling about the slighting joke I just made,
I am confused...
the Mentoring-bloody- Partner says, 'you're not going to be in this class if you keep going at this rate...'

Yes, he would say that...

And what would I say?

No humorous way of saving the situation?

Can't think of anything…I would have to just save face…and get the hell out…

No. Wait…I have seduced the Mentoring Partner…! He is in love with me. And this is how it happens…

He has been in love with me since the time that he first saw me
He knows that we will not 'happen' and he resents that
He tries and tries to harass me about the WIP statement and other administrative crap
Till he knows that he has gone too far.
He feels he has gone too far because of the sheer firmness of character that I display
Because of my strength and unrelenting resolve…!
I am never cornered and he is tired of the game…

So we're in the conference room together
Alone
And he breaks down and owns up
He professes his profound love for me and
grabs me …

I am cold and stare frigidly at him…
He has lost…he knows it isn't worth fighting anymore
He mumbles an apology,
And I forgive him
We become civil again…
He is forever grateful and,

I don't have to worry about the WIP ever again…
Nobody does
Fantastic!

And very unlikely. Maybe I could just hit him and run.

I stand up
And say,
'You are so bloody convinced that your shit don't stink…but
it does, Savvy?'
The last bit said like Clint Eastwood…clenched teeth.
I am chewing a cigar…or something…
How heroic.

Before they escort me out, terminating my employment
with immediate effect.

How depressing. –

           *   *   **

–   *I   walk   a   lonely   road*
The   only   one   that   I   have   ever…   something
Don't   know   where   it   goes
But   it's…something…to   me   and   I   walk   alone

I walk this empty street
On the Bou-le-vard of Broken Dreams
Where the city sleeps
And   I'm   the   something…something…hmm   hmm
I walk alone, I walk alone, I walk alone…um hmmm hmmm

hmmm

Notice how you don't know a single song complete. You don't even know who sang most of them.

At least, I don't. And in a pub, when they start playing this song...we look so bloody excited...connect with the DJ, thank him with our eyes because it is too bloody loud to speak. I lip sync most of it because I am not sure of the words and then suddenly you hear me singing the chorus aloud, along with all the other frauds who suddenly find voices. And the DJ mutes the volume, lets us finish the lyric...of a song that we don't remember...and we feel great, the unison...our collective voice...all of us frauds singing together.

We want to know these songs so we can act like they mean something to us...that we are this cool, hardworking bitch who will climb the corporate ladder but still knows these songs...songs about not caring anymore, walking on the *Boulevard of Broken Dreams*, wherever that may be.

And yes, it not the corporate ladder in my case ergo, replace aforesaid phrase with 'legal ladder'.

I really *do* like this song, though. Why haven't I learnt the lyrics? Learnt to strum the guitar...like I can see myself strumming when I sing the song in my mind...

I sing with my eyes closed, holding my guitar
I walk alone, I walk alone, I walk alone...

they stare and stare at me in awe
passion drips from my face
They love me…but do not have the courage to tell me that.
They are pleading with me to stop walking alone
And choose them as companions…

But I am this sexy, single, rock-star chick and I am wearing
black leather pants and this black leather vest…and I am
singing,
I walk this empty street…

Snap out of it. The street is not empty. The road is not
lonely. It's bloody swarming, really. We are all flies. We
are vermin. The sheer number…

I walk alone, I walk alone, I walk alone… um hmmm hmmm
hmmm…

*   *   *

Of course! Of course!

I can see what happened to him. This is how it
happened.

He lost his job, but he was doing fine
He had taken that mortgage because he was doing just fine…
They talked about it… she said that she was there for him…her
parents would help… they'd take some money from his
brother…'don't worry…we will sail through this…'

'At what cost?'

'At any cost…worse things could happen…'

'Such as?'

The Taliban burning down your house in Pakistan…the Germans treating us like they did the Jews…us seeing our children starve in Africa…the more you think about it…it was just a job! We will be alright…'

His Father-in-Law visited often…

then he gifted his Son-in-Law a copy of 'Who Moved My Cheese?' smiling with great composure, not showing any sympathy…man to man…

They were strong…they would make it…

'But I don't want to make it…like this…' he thinks…the more he hears himself say it… the more he likes to believe it…'like this…like beggars…like desperate men and women…'

His children are lovely, too believing…

They will grow up to know how I lost it all…they will grow up to see that I was laid-off…that I had to be saved…You will lose your patience…'

They will love you for what you did for them…they will not ever be afraid…they would know what a strong father they had…how his faith saw his family through the worst of times…I will always be there for you…you could cook for me, you know?' she smiles at him…

He looks into her eyes…no worry in them yet…
but he will see it one day…
'…not like this…'

Everyone owns a gun in America…he had one too…
He is decided…

'Not like this…'

too many consoling conversations…
things were not going to get any better…he is no fool
He will make them happy… he is no loser…
he still makes the decisions …
he shoots his son in the back of his head while he watched Winnie the Pooh on television…
somewhere in the house, there is panicked response to the sound…
his daughter is in the next room…
he smiles at her, holding the gun behind his back…
'I want to show you something…let's look outside the window…'

'Being shot at is like diving into cold water'… he had read that somewhere…
Her young red blood splatters across the window pane and the curtains…he holds her close…looking into her fading eyes, 'My baby! I love you so much…'

He cannot waste time on tears…this is not sad…they will all be together soon.

He sees her at the door… shrieking in denial of what was meant to be…
there are other voices in the house…
'Oh! We have visitors again…' he cannot waste a second…
He shoots her in the chest looking into her shocked eyes…
She is flung across the sofa, falls on her back…

He reaches her but she is not looking at him...she is looking across the room, past the door, at her dead little girl...

He looks up to see that his in-laws are upon him and shoots them too...
'Why did I do that...?'
He shoots himself...'Not like this...'

He had made a sacrifice! Wow!

I have my story! I have it! I have it! I have it! –

She has her phone handy, "Hullo? Hi...again...AJ!"

"Yeeeeeeees...! Tell me!"

"First, why are you receiving my calls, AJ? After months of not answering them. Are you or are you not at work? Do you want to be laid-off?"

He laughs. "I am not at work, Meera. I wanted to tell you something even when we were on the phone last night but, it isn't important. You to go first."
"I'm curious now! I just...I wanted to tell you that I think I found my story."

"You're not going with the Pakistani-blowing-up-a-bus?"

"No...we're done with the 9/11 empathize-with-a-terrorist-shit...there is more happening now...the economy…did you read about the suicide in the papers this morning?"

"Yes…"
"That's the inspiration…your Federal Reserve stimulus Package of last night did not help him. Maybe he never found out about it. You see, he was 'Making a Sacrifice'…"

"Okay…I think I could like that."

"You get it, right? You know…the paper was just lying at my desk this morning…I don't even know who put it there…and then I saw the Post-It reminder…it all fits in…very inspiring and all! Like it was meant to be…but you are just not the right person to discuss these things with…you're always encouraging and positive …and, you never criticize the idea or anything…"

"I don't criticize because there is nothing submitted to me for my perusal, young lady! Give me the work and see me go! Don't ever say this again…"

"Right. Whammy. Your turn to tell all."

"I'm going away for a bit…"

"Going away? Where to?"

"I'm going to Ladakh. Call it a vacation. Just time out. Headed to a monastery out there."

"A monastery? Priests? Buddhists."

"Yes. Just retiring for a bit to silence and thought."

"Can I come?"

"Sure. Carry Baby along. That should give them peace and quiet!" he laughs.

"This is something…that's why you're not at work? That's why you were on such a bloody long call with me last night."

"Yep. Took a sabbatical."

"Wow! And you tell me now? Why didn't you tell me when we watched *Savior*? God! I have been selfish and self-obsessed…you're obviously *not* alright! How are you, darling?"

"I'm fine! I really am. I'm not going to be cut-off or anything. I can take calls out there so you could track me down when you have your sudden ideas. And, did he die in the end? Quaid?"

"No, he lived. Screw the movie, AJ. I was supposed to be taking time off today, to be with my thoughts, to understand them but I am talking to you and I went to the office where I wasted the day. I want to run away too!"

"I'm not *running* away. I am taking a break. Big difference. And, talking to me *is* the same as you speaking with yourself. Do that as often as you can."

"Sure...you talk to me as often as possible, don't you? That's why we spoke after what, two months last night? And I learn of your plans like this. Second, I don't see the difference between taking a break and running away. What's wrong with *running* away? I wish that there were other worlds out there. Worlds not premised on the frivolous falsehoods of this one...You know, I got rammed at work and as we speak the others must be suffering the same or worse ordeal. They are consolidating and all and I don't understand it, they won't let us be...we are not *innocent* anymore...there is no camaraderie...just one-upmanship...I know that they have to do this...it is business...but we are professionals, not factory men. I want to give up ...I'm tired of faking it...you know it is really weird to sit through these meetings when you have a pretty lively fetus dancing around in your tummy...What *am* I doing here? What was I *ever* doing here? And why? For the money, you would say...and I know that...but why has it not stopped being important to me? Why do I live this falsehood and aim to comply with its rules? Why can't I walk away?"

"I agree. It's a bloody charade and I am done with it. I want to start something of my own, be my own worker, my own boss, my own employee. That is the only way I will survive this world."

"So you are all set…looking for inspiration in the mountains…! You know, the clean air of the mountains clears your head…you will return knowing exactly what you want…till you realize that you don't want it anymore."

"One *has* to go that far when one fails to find inspiration in the newspapers lying on one's desk!"

She has to laugh at that. "Right! You are making a sacrifice!"

"How is that?"

"You won't know what it was like out here, in this shithole, while you were out there…"

"Oh! You meant it like that! No, I am not making a sacrifice, I'm making a discovery."

"Yes. I suppose you are…I will not know what it was like out *there*…I am making a sacrifice."
"Till you do eventually go there…once you have published your work and can walk away from things…"

"Once I have even started creating my work…"

"I think it is alright for you to make the said sacrifice, given the cause…Glory is yours for the taking…!"

"Hmmm, Alexander…"

"I am Alexander…"

"Yah! Buddhist, non-violent, Gimme-Peace-Alexander!"

"I am off this week-end. And I will see you when I see you and all that."

"This is Goodbye?"

"For now. But it doesn't mean that you cannot call me when you arrive at a major postulate, this day of all others, I am at your disposal!"

"So sweet of you! Alexander is obliged to you, Hephaestion…I think we will speak again…and oh! *Om Mani Padme Hum.*"

"What was that?"

"Luck. And success on your journey and everything else that I could wish for you and all. It is a Tibetan, Buddhist *mantra.*"

"Thanks, Freako. Sweet. Call me, okay?"

*   *   *

– I want to cry. He is going away…*flying* away…and it should be me!

I can fly when I want to…

Why don't I lift off the ground?

What am I doing walking down this crowded, ugly street in Ballard Estate where the cabs don't stop honking…?

This clink and clang of crowded life readying itself for a greasy lunch? These old buildings that are the stuff of tourist's photographs that stare down at the crappy new constructions around them, all walls that hold me in. Prison walls that I will not surmount.

Where do I go from here? I have to walk now…on the *Boulevard of Broken Dreams*…because I cannot fly…–

*   *   *

– I need *chai*.

From the vendor at VT.

It is really cool and all to be drinking tea at a *tapri* but I am past that. In fact, I feel sorry for those guys hanging around that pathetic street stall sipping that sick tea.

Where the stall owner has only place enough for his tower of not-washed-with-soap-just-rinsed-with-filthy-water glasses piled one into the other and that jar of stale biscuits made in cheap oil, *dalda*, or whatever that is - pig fat, maybe - instead of butter.

The vendor smiles a happily proud smile because he sees himself telling his slum-mates how he cooks tea for the well-dressed *saabs and memsaabs* of Ballard Estate, or Nariman Point or BKC or wherever. His smile is a fake smile that he puts on because he knows that his customers feed on his purported excitement at having them surround him. Their bonus for suffering a pathetic beverage.

Compromised standards. Those stalls, they use rat milk.

Funny aftertaste to the funny tasting, funny smelling tea. I could puke.

VT tea is alright. Dip tea, not my first choice, but he uses milk. Indian Railways-sanctioned-watery-milk, not whitener, not rat milk.

Standard stuff. –

*   *   *

She crosses the road at the Ballard Estate Post Office refusing to admire the quaint architectural wonder distracted instead by the monstrosities that surround it, the monstrosities that surround her. She looks at them in hateful awe.

– I cannot always find the oasis...sometimes, just sometimes, I must revel in the negativity of it all, the ugliness, ugly wretchedness of it all...

Why must I be happy in moderation? And then, cry controlled tears?

I want to sink deep down into the sea...swim through its despondency...

That rhymed...

I am as I was made to be
Man, prone to treachery
Mortal, I make merry...
Prone to err, and to pardon
Another flower from Adam's garden...

Write that down...or don't, because you can't while you're crossing the road. But don't forget it...please! –

*   *   *

At the crossing, she waits for the light to turn green. She is standing with another woman.

– oh great! She is pregnant too. –

They smile at each other. The light turns green. The woman walks briskly away.

– she has a train to catch. She will head home and cook for her husband and maybe other kids, maybe her in-laws. She has to get a seat on that train. It would be uncomfortable to stand all the way.

Her tummy is all covered with that awesome long stole that we use for everything…

She has slung her *dupatta* on her right shoulder and is holding its folds across her tummy in her left hand…as if the *dupatta* across her tummy will protect its roundness from the Evil Eye…as if she were embarrassed to be pregnant…her clothes are loose.

I guess you should be embarrassed…I mean, when you dress the way I am, it is like holding a sign…big sign, saying, 'DID IT… SOME TIME BACK'.

That was the first thing I thought of as a kid when I saw a pregnant woman, 'hey… she did it'.

And then I'd want to look at her husband…I could wonder about what it was like when they did it…

But now I have learnt to smile the way we just did at each other. Positive. Happy. Mature. Knowing. Pure. *Conspiring?*

An individual, who errs and pardons
Another flower from Adam's garden…

You cannot stop the mind. It runs free…

So…Let it.

Don't stop…

I am walking towards the Life Insurance Building…
Summer break
I believe that I will come to work here…
This is the place for the ambitious…this is the place for pace…
The internship's been good…maybe they will make me an offer?

I've gotten off the train at Churchgate station on my way to work…
I feel this presence…not a supernatural presence…around me…
where is it?
Behind me…

asshole of a puny ass of a man sticking to me…
I push him away…

no change of expression
in spite of the sensational expletives that accompany the shove.
too busy to hear what I have been saying about his suspect lineage…

He heads to another woman who got off the ladies' compartment…
I follow the sick bastard…have to figure what he is up to…is he a pickpocket?
I am not afraid…this is Bombay. The station is alive with the morning rush hour.

Then, he moves smoothly away…
To another woman…then another…they are all walking briskly to work…
after that sickly, sweaty nap in the train…they are a little bit delirious and don't notice him right away…
what is he doing? I cannot make out…
I can only see his head and shoulders through the crowd of heads and shoulders…
The crowd clears. I see him…
He is holding his puny penis…stretching it real hard and far through his open zipper…
not far, it can't go too far…

He is touching the clothes, bags, purses, sarees, dupattas…
anything that the women may have with them or on them…
he is careful not to touch them with any other part of his body
he has his pelvis stuck out and walks funny with his knees bent.
Can nobody else see him?

He is touching all that with his PRICK! That is his fetish…

I reach for my behind to check if it is wet or something…
maybe he is peeing on all of us…
Marking his territory. fucking dog…
nothing on me…

Asshole perverts are like a box of chocolates, you never know what you're gonna get…

Run! Forrest! Run!

The thing about crowds – cramped humanity.

The collective stink that it throws up – of their households, queues for toilets in their *chawls*, the clutter of their lives, chatter and cacophony from their loud television sets, all boil together in the crowd.

Ugly as the crowd may be, you see its beauty…unlike the deceiving beauty of an oasis…yes, the beauty of the truth…naked, very ugly and calming.

The truth that you are part of this crowd, its collective stink…its noise.

You are no one. You are everyone.

The depressing, collective, blatant, anonymity of the men and women in the crowd…hits you like a wet sock on your face…and it hits hard…

Here I stand. They pass me by…just another woman in the crowd…

'just a face among a million faces…just another woman with no name'

I am not even that, *Nina! Pretty Ballerina!*
I am not unique.

I am not going to propound a great legal theory. I am not going to win a landmark case. Hell. I am not even trying. I have no secrets. I am not mysterious. I am pretty. But then, most women are. I have put on weight. I will not lose it. I am not hugely successful. I am not a notable failure. I will be a mother and will try really hard to get nowhere.

I will die quite friendless because I stay in a big, ugly, Indian city and it is difficult to keep in touch with people. I am not special. I am not unique. I am the crowd.

This is where you should come to when you are down and out, even when you are up and about!

This is real.

A lesson in humility...the crowd at the Victoria Terminus...no, *Chatrapati Shivaji* Terminus...a lesson in relevance, the relevance of your fears, joys, sadness, your face, dreams, memories, imagination, your story...and their absolute nothingness.
The trouble with tea at VT - no place to sit and drink it.

Why should there be?

Is it fair to ask for a fragment of peace in this hub representing the confluence of everything that there is...and isn't?

I cannot sit on the steps like I used to...clumsy. I'll get unwanted attention... preggers, sitting on the steps...well-dressed woman...what's with her? Has she lost it? Or worse, 'What's wrong with her, did she fight with her husband?'

And that'll be it. They will not wait to hear me answer.

They will not wait to know that I'm cool, just enjoying my cuppa...I will be written off. And then, forgotten in the rush for trains... –

She steps out of VT, her paper cup in hand, sipping the tea before she takes the stairs. She has decided that between the McDonald's opposite VT, and the Barista near Sterling Cinema, she prefers the latter. It means that she will have to get a coffee or one of their fancy teas if she has to sit there but she does not ditch the cup in her hand just yet.

She waddles down the stairs of the subway refusing to join the jaywalkers who swarm the treacherous crossing outside the terminus.

*   *   *

– this is comfortable.

When you can afford it, you should. The five rupees VT tea is alright and all but this is...cozy.

I like the way they have used the space outside.

I don't like the guitar with broken strings and that it still hangs on the wall. It depresses me. The way that the broken strings are looped into the three remaining strings…

I can imagine how this happened, how it became this pathetic, limp…sad, joke. I *know* how it happened…

pseudo college kids walk in and decide to bash the instrument…
the girls giggle uncontrollably…
The boys look at the guitar and the guy who holds it but cannot play…
they are jealous of the effect that he is having on the girls…
They grab at the guitar as if it was the one girl among them…
the rough handling snaps a string or two…
they are neither embarrassed nor guilty but look around pretending they are worried about whether anyone saw them do it…
the girls - they cover their mouths because their teeth are ugly…
their shoulders are pulled in and up…
so they look small and pretty

they split some coffees and cakes between themselves, while the guitar stands leaning on their table, its broken strings sprawled on the floor like a broken man.
The staff cleans up after them, looping the broken strings around the remaining three loose crutch-strings - a bid at warped aesthetics.

They hang it up for me to look at and cry about
I can hear those criminals giggling still…

I have to write something…anything…focus on 'Making a Sacrifice' for now… mundane…tell a story about the mundane…
These are going to be Gogh's paintings. No one will buy them…
So what?

The five thousand words limit. What about that? How is even half to be achieved? It will not be good enough to compete.

Why worry about that? Act on it …

Write only because that is what I want to do?

Do you! Do you really want to write?

Yes…I do…I do.

I should have started this years ago…carrying my notebook with me everywhere.

It should be my soulmate…I will not forget…I will carry it with me. I will not forget now…

I have to pee…
to pee blissfully feeling the gush…
panicked frenzy, climax…
orgasmic rush…
subsiding into relieved peacefulness…

is not possible even at Barista in spite of the number of foreigner footfalls…
Not enough toilet paper… –

She covers the spider-web-like-cracked toilet seat with two layers of paper, which soak in the assorted urine, cleaning chemical and splashed water till the paper-layers cling to the seat. She pinch-lifts the paper holding a dry corner that is soaking fast.

– to this extent, we are all obliged to be Gandhian once in a while…us women. At some point or the other, we clean the community's potties.

And why do we do it? Why! To be able to take a disease-free pee…but it is hopeless, impossible to clean.

I will squat hovering my inner thighs and bottom an inch over that seat, at risk of the apparatus coming loose… baby and all… target receptacle…drop some of my own into the wizened cracks of the sticky potty-seat… leaving my mark with everyone else's…An overwhelming, primitive, feeling of union with the Universe…the public toilet in India…

Boy! I needed this! –

She finds her Mocha at the table and this time, sits with her back to the broken guitar on the wall.

– mocha sucks!

Sugar…more…lots more…focus…now:

<u>'Making a Sacrifice'</u>
<u>(last shot at said theme)</u>

<u>A Birthday Party - Done Differently</u>

*'I want to do something different for Tuk's birthday this time,'
declared Mrs. S at lunch on Sunday afternoon. 'If Tuk is
alright with it, I'd like to keep things simple this time!'
continued Mrs. S looking kindly at her daughter and then
back into her plate for inspiration in her half-eaten food.*

'Simple?' thought Tuk. 'What's wrong with Mom?'

*'I want to, or wanted to, do something that my Grandmother
would do for us, a feast for the poor. But only if this is
acceptable to all of us, only if we all agree!'*

'But my friends are not poor.'

*'Of course they aren't, darling. For them we will do a lovely
lunch but before your birthday.'*

*Tuk saw the light here. Her birthday would be so, so special
that it could not involve them! They would only have to hear
her stories about how it all had turned out! It would be
exciting and mysterious.*

'We are not interested in crass displays of flamboyance, are we? We are not interested in feeding the overfed and ordering extravagant snacks for guests who only eat with their eyes.'

Both his women turned to Mr. S. 'You don't think it would be easier to get one of those event managers to take over and be done with the whole thing? She can always feed the poor later on…?' was what he said.

No.

No, they were both convinced that this would be a pleasant change from the manner in which birthdays were celebrated these days. It would be traditional. Some close friends and relatives could make it a full house.

'What about these 'poor' people? Where will you find them?' continued the skeptic Mr. S.

'Oh! The servants and their families, of course! I will also speak to the night guard about bringing them over.'

Tuk would wear a simple cotton dress so that her special young guests did not feel bad.

The thought of the grateful looks that she would receive from those starved eyes as she served them food and drink like they had never before tasted kept Tuk awake all night. She would be their Fairy Godmother.

Mrs. S was expecting anywhere between fifty to seventy children in batches of ten to twelve. She had made little packets for all of them – their return gifts. Lots of sweets, some toys and a Hundred Rupee note in each packet.

They started trickling in at the appointed time and sat in a row on the floor.

The caterers carried massive bowls of food into the drawing room and Tuk stood there happily ready to serve the quietly seated children. When they were done they picked up their disposable plates and put them in the dustbin. Tuk peered into their faces. They had not looked at her at all. They walked with their heads bowed.

When they made a quiet queue near the door without being asked to do so, Mrs. S called out to Tuk to hand over their return gifts, which lay piled-up on a table.

Tuk was Santa Claus, her Uncles clicked photographs and her Aunts gathered around smiling. And, the next batch of children waiting outside moved in.

'Mummy! None of them even wished me! They are not smiling… and they did not thank us!'

'They do not have the benefit of your schooling and good home, darling. Be kind.'

It was the same with the next lot. Tuk handed the spoon to the caterers and went into her room to open the presents that she had received from her friends.

When she stepped out of her room after a short nap, Tuk found that the crowd in her house had only grown. There were those ugly, dark children again!

Her mother spoke animatedly with an Aunt. The waves of children entering her home were turning into a tsunami. Surely, there had been more than thirty extra children already? The return gifts were all over...and they would definitely run out of food very soon! How had this happened?

The Aunt would tell off the little guests at the door.

'Oh! God! The poor children will feel so bad!'

'Now really, we are all feeling bad...but what can one do?'

'Okay. Okay. Go tell them that there is no more food! God! I cannot get myself to do it...'

The cooking maid helped convincing the waiting children that they must leave. They know her for she is one of the Aunties who live in their slum.

In the evening, the tired family sat together in the drawing room while the caterers noisily wrapped up for the day.

Mr. S settled the payments and the tips when the doorbell rang. Tuk rushed expectantly to the door and opened it to the building's watchmen.

'What do they want?' asked the tired Mrs. S.

Mr. S asks his wife to rest in her room instructing Tuk to join her there. But Mrs. S sits at the dining table looking anxiously towards the door and at her husband. Mr. S mumbles softly, his wife cannot hear what the men outside the door are saying because he holds the door so close to himself, as if hiding his family from them. He hands the waiting men a bundle of cash and shuts the door.

Mrs. S frowns at her husband, 'Why did you give them so much money?'

'They wanted the taxi fares for having transported all those children to our place…' he sounds nonchalant.

Mrs. S chokes, covering her mouth as if she was going to throw-up, she walks briskly into her room, where they hear her break down, crying.

Tuk looks at her father, her eyes welling up. He resignedly carries his daughter into the weeping woman's room.

Mrs. S turns to them. 'We will never do this again! I am so sorry. It was such a waste.'

Those slum dwellers, the watchmen, had made a sacrifice.

Not the last bit. It should be obvious, shouldn't it? It's not like this is a fable with a moral and all…you can't end with 'they had made a sacrifice' and stuff … –

Meera scratches out the last sentence that she wrote and calmly turns the pages, tweaking here and there, with notes in the margins.

CHAPTER 3
AFTERNOON

– I like short stories.

Episodic insights into lives. Life and living. The really important stuff, concisely put.

A quickie.

My times, my generation. A short story.

From the writer's perspective, the story finishes before you can write yourself into a corner. Before you come up against that insurmountable mountain of rock – the writers' block.

Yes. I like short stories. –

*   *   *

3 P.M. She steps out of the coffee shop.

Where to from here? Sandwich and some cake at Kayani's. A leisurely long walk before the crowd going home fills up the streets! Awesome…I cannot believe I skipped lunch. Wasn't I hungry? Did the coffee fill me up?

How do people *live* on this pavement? Where do they come from? They sleep in the afternoon… My God! All of them are sleeping! Like a pavement dorm. They will cook in the late evening once the last wave of pedestrian-crowd has gone home and left the footpath to them. They will cook in a large, black pot, a mix of all that they have managed for the day. With fat, thick and hard *rotis* so that they know the pleasure of chewing. Nothing like the soft, fluffy 'Indian breads' that I get served at home and in restaurants.

Don't they ever want to go back, like in *The Good Earth*? To their villages and farms?

Look at the women…dark, with matted hair and children at their breasts.

Voluptuous.

Where do they get those colourful, backless, peek-a-boo blouses tailored? How much does it cost? They fit really well.

They don't wear bras. Look at their old women and you're sure that they do not.

And the men...thin spindles...sinewy muscles...from lifting heavy weights...sacks...garbage, maybe. Or from pulling heavy carts. Like the cycle rickshaw drivers' muscles.

But you would not sleep with them even if lean bodies, dark chiseled jaws and pronounced collar bones turned you on.

We are very clean in India.

I don't understand the social structures of the West. How the hell do they sleep with gardeners? And milkmen and what not.

There are no standards there or maybe the standard is bloody high...of the average man on the street...I mean, if the gardener looked like Brad Pitt, sure...I would understand. Assuming also that the fellow bathed frequently enough.

Their kids are cute. Brown hair.

Ginger. And dark bodies. Like the parents'. Sometimes they beg.

Ginger hair because it is bleached in the crazy sun...their stomachs are pot-bellied... they have Kwashiorkor.

Or whatever that protein deficiency disease was. Learnt it in Class 10. They should have brought us here...to the footpath opposite VT and St. Xavier's college and all...

'See? This is Kwashiorkor.
Now, I don't want you spelling it wrong in the examination!'
says the Teacher while the students stare and stare...

And I can see the parents fuming at the nasty lesson that was taught too soon...I can see the teacher being reprimanded for her teaching methods...

Yep.

That's why they never take you to the slum during practical study. Too much. Too soon. And all.

I mean, you want to learn about absent birth control, you see it there.

You want to learn about absent hygiene and rodents, you have it all...this is the place for serious students of pretty much any subject.

Except History. Or Art. Or Math.

No, why? Of course, maybe some form of statistics. And oh! Yes! The History of urbanization. Some socio-political crap. Or just *their* histories. Their collective History. Who'd have the time for their individual histories? Awesome for art students, too.

The kind of art that shocks you…the kind that looks for beauty in ugliness…Goya's art. Good for the arty-farty types to rave on and on about.

Goya's Ghosts. The Potato Eaters. And then, *The Pavement Dwellers.* Ta dah!

It *is* Kwashiorkor. Protein deficiency? Calcium deficiency? There was another one that I am forgetting.

It's called something else in adults. And one thing in kids.

No. That was Osteoporosis versus Rickets. Ten mark question. If you divided the differences under 5 clear heads, you got a ten-on-ten. Two per…

How do they…? Where do they give birth? In this mess?

Government hospital.

Of course.

Hmmm…where do they do it, then? Bombay never sleeps. And this is one of the main arteries connecting Fort and Colaba and Cuffe Parade with the rest of the world…except sea-routes, of course…when do they do it?
In the night?

No afternoon fornication for them. No midday sex.

I can see them, hear them…remember what it is like to see them fight …like… cocks…like cats and dogs…cats and dogs is a truer description, I think.

the women held him back from beating her up
some women screamed at her and held her back from beating him up…
The men kept their distance from the scene…
Older kids watched them amusedly.
The babies had cried…
Because they had awakened - from their peaceful sleep amidst the familiar sounds of cars, taxis, buses and blaring car horns to the horrid sound of these warring, screaming adults…

The short, thin, chisel-muscled-boned man …
And the delicately chisel-muscled-boned, woman…
Both of equally dark skin darkened shiny black because of the sun they live under…
Howl at each other.
Passersby ignore them
they know that the pavement dwellers only look like they could kill each other…
that the worst that may happen is someone getting hurt…
You cannot make out their language…
It is not a language…
That is too wholesome a word for what the pavement dwellers speak…
It is a dialect, maybe…a north-Indian village version of Hindi.
But if you listen carefully, from his and her intonation

you can make out exactly when, in their runny sentences, they abuse each other…

The language of abuse is Universal…

The change of rhythm in their voices …

a static-sporadic sound, a convulsion in conclusion of, or intermittent to, the argument…

the spit-showering abuse…

their expressions become free from reason –no logic to what they will say next

they say it as if to themselves…

yelling, uncertain mouths become sure because they are going to say the things that they have heard most…

their wild gesticulations are in sync with the static-sporadic words spit-showered out of their convulsing mouths…

that is when you know that they are abusing…

yes, and some of the abuses are familiar…

they refer to body parts and are accompanied by actions that have few synonyms…

Like that of Love…

The language of Hate is Universal.

Then, it is late at night

So late that it could be morning…

She is sleeping with the children around her…

He goes over to her and gruffly touch-pushes her shoulder. He walks on.

She knows what this is.

She rises up slowly, purposely…

They walk away together…where to?

Across the road? Near the Xavier's campus boundary wall? Maybe…

Because I don't think any of them sleep on that side of the road…

*yes, that is correct. All the settlements are on this side of the
road...*
It could be agreement, tacit understanding...
*The Xavier's side is for defecating towards the outer footpath,
so that the feces fall on the road*
And the rest of the footpath for...other bodily functions...
*Or maybe, they head for the Metro subway steps...but those
aren't really secluded spots...you could be surprised by a
drunk pedestrian who will totter home late...*
or surprise him.
*Maybe he has a setting with the Azad Maidan guards...and
they enter a secluded spot in that field, which in the morning
is used for games, political rallies,*
festive fetes and other forms of power-play...

Some of their neighbours see them leave
But there must be a basic respect for human need
that you develop when you live like this...
No lewd comments...everyone knows
*And the neighbours don't say anything that they wouldn't
want said when they walk away like this...*
Do unto others...and all that

*Anyway, the two of them don't take off their clothes...just
loosen strings and buttons...*
They forget about their lives, their issues and
that they could be hungry because the food was not enough...
Are they capable of love...?
*I mean, when she lies down on the muddy, filthy ground with
him on top...*

And his rough hands balk
at the softness of her breasts and inner arms and inner thighs...
does he think her beautiful?
Does he know what that means? Beautiful.
Is she satisfied? Or would she have preferred foreplay? Does she know what that means?
They look at each other fleetingly...
They are not fools...they are not one and all that...this is not a union...
all that spiritual stuff.
They are two human beings satisfying each other's need...because nobody else will.
And this is one need at least, that stands a shot at satisfaction.

– do they love? Their families...?

Their numbers only increase...so do the number of pets that they keep...*can* they love?

It is pouring
The pavements flood with run-off
Along the edges
Along the middle
Water is everywhere, flooding the cracks and crevices of the cobbled footpath.
And you are surprised that the pavement slopes in the odd directions that it does because of the way in which the water flows.
The decrepit boundary walls that they sling their clothes across are also wet like one long, leaking clothes hanger
They wear damp clothes on their damp bodies.
The rain rains from above

Then massive puddles and drowning drains spill over with
dark water...
The sky and the ground
are both wet.
Their cloth tents are buffered with blue tarpaulin...but that
cannot save them from the run-off on the pavement.
So they sleep on planks laid on bricks and the flat stones that
they could find.

This man's blanket is touching the pavement
I can see the water slowly soaking into the
dark-brown-filthy-black-rough-but-warm-fabric.
He snuggles with a dog.
The dog's fur is matted and drops of rain-water sparkle on
him, waiting to spring-off when he shakes himself dry
He likes the comfortable feel of a live human body.
The cats don't cuddle...but they share the food.
And I see what I see...
Sinewy muscles, like the rest of them, under his full old-white
shirt I am sure he has the same collar bones...
I look for his thin chiseled legs...
I find just one...one leg
I am alert now and find his crumbling old crutch, padded with
rags
so that it does not bruise his armpits.
And at his foot, is his pet dog just woken up, shaking himself
dry, ears flapping on his doggybrown cheeks,
A shiver rolling down his doggy spine till it fades away at his
tail...
He hops into the rain on three doggy legs.

For a moment, I am overcome
with the nauseating thought that this was arranged on
purpose…
That dog was maimed to look like man so that the
unsuspecting pedestrian
feels responsible for the grand irony that jumps at his
unsuspecting conscience, snapping it out of its petty woes and
devices…

You can forget what you see
by dropping loose change into a begging bowl that accepts
such a bribe…

But they are not begging…

What does love mean to them? How does it drive them? Can it be compared with the love in *our* families?

These people are worse off than the slum dwellers.

Maybe that is their ambition…? To become a slum dweller. To be able to afford a house in this or that slum. To be able to rent a place there.

Do they have ambitions? What does a young pavement dwelling teen plan for himself?

I don't see them staring wistfully at me.

The way that I am staring at them, the way that I am imagining their lives, their love-making…

That's right. They are oblivious to my riches. They don't imagine my house. They can't. They've never seen anything like it. No movies. No picture books. No insight. No perspective.

We are parallel worlds and the species of one can see and feel the other but the other does not know. They cannot know.

My species is the voyeuristic one. Their species does not look past the imaginary wall of their open-for-all-to-see pavement dwelling. They sit comfortably on the filthy pavement, cross-legged, chatting, oblivious to the sound of traffic, oblivious to my hungrily prying eyes.

Are they happy?

Am I happy?

Not for just this moment. Ignore all the stuff you complain about. Ignore the reasons for unhappiness that you would list for yourself.

Are you happy? If yes, list your reasons for being happy.

Are there *reasons* for being happy? Just happy. Just alright, good? Do there have to be...reasons?

Or like love, do you just *know*?

I am happy.

Why? Do you think yourself happy because you see these people on the street not looking wistfully at you?

No. They don't look wistfully at me because they are happy…in a way that I will not pretend to understand.

I am happy because I can imagine a part of their lives without wanting to exchange mine for theirs…I don't think I am looking wistfully at them, either. What does wistful *mean* anyway? I am not longing for their lives. I guess, I *long* to know what their lives are like and I am not *longing* to become them or anything *like* them. I think. Yes. Yes, that's what I am thinking.

To me, these street dwellers are specimens from another world. An uglier world than mine is. They don't worry about riches. They worry about other stuff. Everyone worries about something. Even if you give it all up, you'll worry about finding the right cave to retire to.

They don't look happier than the next man on the street. They don't look sad.

They have nothing to do with my being happy. With my belief that I am happy.

No? But you have been griping all day.

I mean, seeing these people may have prompted the realization that I am not really unhappy. That I was just thinking thoughts. Complaining thoughts. And that just because things could be better doesn't mean that they are bad. –

She shakes her head silencing the arguing voices in there and reaches for her phone.

"Debbie? Hi! How are you and where?"
"I am at home. Hi, Meera! Where are you?"

"Outside your house, if you want to call it that…I am just crossing the road from Xavier's to Metro. Can we meet? I need you to do something for me…"

"You are at Metro?"

"Yes."

"Why didn't you tell me you were coming?"

"I would tell you that I wanted to surprise you. The truth however, is that I was walking and just happened to find myself here. I actually wanted to hit Kayani's for some sandwiches but the familiar stink of this place has turned me off. I am going to get a sandwich or something from a better place after I get you to do something for me."
"What?"

"Will that determine whether you come down to meet me or not?"

"No."

"Great! So move fast because I am not coming up to that stinking shithole you stay in and meeting your landlady and all…"

"She was your landlady too before you got whisked off to that palace in Colaba…"

"Palace? What palace? Come. Come!"

*   *   *

– she is short. Tubby.

Her skin is smooth, flawless, neither fair nor dark… *saawanli*, they would call her – like the monsoon. Or maybe…wheatish.

Is that even a word? Is that a colour? Wheatish? Brown, like wheat.

Is there an international registry of colours?

Wheatish, not to be confused with ochre.

I liked ochre from the moment I heard its name – *ochre*.

It was almost the only colour I used in art class. My art teacher did not really notice because she was too busy being surprised at how terrible my work was. But I did become very good at painting trees, and leaves. Got the colours right.

'You create the feel of the trunk, the bark and branches
and the leaves look so real. I am waiting for them to flutter!'
I am amazed that she bothered to say this to me
She is easily the best living artist I ever knew
I am so obsessed with how she looks that in my mind, I become her
I have that same smooth skin,
not a facial hair to be seen except for the fuzz when you were so close that
she thought you were engrossed in the painting that she was making and
not in fact staring at her cheek and the gentle curve of her chin, wondering at the absent side-burns...
I start to see bronze in my own hair
I make herbal hair packs with heaps of turmeric powder for a tint of yellow
I adopt her gentle mannerisms,
which make me look uglier than I know...
I ask her about it - her skin and her hair
She tells me that her grandmother was French and that she looks like her.
I feel cheated and relieved at the same time...
Of course! French! No wonder I did not have what she had!
So she liked my painting...the trees and the leaves...
I cannot have that skin and that hair.
I shrug it off saying, 'I use a lot of ochre...'

Debbie has the same skin as her. So I like Debbie's skin. Also, Debbie is Indian. Hardcore Bengali. No French ancestry.

I guess when you are past adolescence you realize that your skin looks alright on you. So I don't want Debbie's skin.

Do men find Debbie pretty?

I do, I mean...because I know her and I am used to her.

But she is not your stereotypical beauty...short and tubby and cute and plump and real. I worry about her. Because I want her to be so happy...because she deserves it and I worry about people not getting what they deserve. –

"Hi!" she shrieks more excited on seeing me than she was when we spoke. "You're looking so cute!"

– that is why you like your female friends. They remind you of girly stuff and girly talk...they remind you of your youth.

Of when you were just starting out.

If I think about it anymore, I will sound like Sarah Jessica Parker and the *Sex and the City* chicks and I don't think that it would be real anymore so I'm going to stop gloating about girlfriends.

You cannot describe it. This feeling that I am feeling. It isn't about brands and finding love. No. Too bloody shallow.

She is not letting me think!

She talks too much and too damned fast…–

"In the last week of December was what the doctor said last…so next month! How the hell have you been? You know, let's go to Kayani's after all!"

 "Alright!"

"I am all by myself these two days…"

"Wow! You know…I have been thinking about you and meaning to call you…"

"That's alright. You are busy and I like to pretend that I am busy…so I have just been walking around, sorting things out…"
"I wanted to ask you something…would it be alright if I came over and stayed for a couple of days with you."

– she's kidding me, right? *Stay with me? And my husband?* In that one bedroom apartment!

I am shopping for the wedding

Nani asks me, 'Are any of your friends coming for the wedding, Beta?'
I say yes, ignoring her loss of context because we are not discussing the guest list…
because I am trying on the red and white Chanderi silk that I did eventually pick up…
'My mother used to tell me, you should never let your girlfriends come too close to the family. Don't talk to them about your husband, don't ever let them come over and stay with you…'

She has my attention. I laugh at her innocent grandmotherly blabbering. 'Is it okay to let the boys come over?'
She does not react, she has said her piece.

her head bobs and wiggles, like a baby's, at the sarees laid resplendently before us…
her head does not bob because it will be strong one day, or because her developing neck will hold her head straight, and up…
could be the onset of Parkinson's…I look at her hands
they don't quiver…steady still
just old age…I think, relieved

That is why Debbie called it a 'palace'! She wants to come over and stay in it…

As if…! –

"Hey!" she snaps her fingers in my face. "Did you hear me?"

"Yes! Yes of course! Listen, why don't you come over for today and tomorrow when he is not around...I think that would be more comfortable and all."

"Okay! That's alright...I'll come over in the evening unless you want to wait for me while I pack?"

– horror! –

"No! I have a lot to do. Make it late evening. Not before dinner, okay?"

"Yah. But I have to get out at a time that doesn't make Aunty ask me a dozen questions so I will have to get out at 8:30 at least."

"8:45."

"Fine! What do you want?"

"*Brun-muska* and tea. And I want the *mawa* cake too."

"Hey! I thought the familiar stink of the place put you off? And, I will have the same," she grins at me, heading for the counter to place her order because the service is terrible and you must pay before you are served.

*   *   *

"So Aunty is still stuck up on timings and all?"

"She will die stuck up…"

"Hmmm…why do you want to come over anyway?"

"You will not believe this, but the house is swarming with bed bugs."

"What?"

"I cannot sleep…they are everywhere. My bag, my shoes, my clothes, my mattress… yesterday, I was so embarrassed, I was speaking to my friends in the college canteen and suddenly I felt one on my arm. I brushed it off before anyone saw it. It is the most demeaning thing I have ever done…Where do we live? What kind of place do they run? The mattress is full of them! I am bitten all over."

"Does she not sun the mattresses?"

"Where is the place? Anyway, she is going to do a pest control tomorrow morning and they have promised that it will be effective. I don't want to be there in that stink so I am really lucky that you are alone."

– sometimes you just have to say what you are thinking. You cannot keep all of your thoughts to yourself always… –

"Listen, Deb, don't take this the wrong way but, I cannot afford to have bugs or any disease carriers in my house at this time…ok? This is tough, *yaar*."

"Hey! I thought about this okay and I was going to my cousin's place but that is too far from college. I really did keep this in mind when I thought of coming over to you…"

– it is amazing how honestly two friends can talk… or two enemies…–

"I have given some clothes to the laundry. I will not carry anything else over," she lowers her voice to a whisper, "except very clean *undies* washed in Dettol, okay?"

"I don't know, girl. What about your shoes and socks and hair and…? This is weird."
"No! It is not weird. It is alright to be frank with me. But I promise that I will be totally clean, okay?"

"Fine! Fine. I will see you in the evening. Now, how is everything else?"
"All good. And you? Have you heard from AJ at all?"

"AJ is going to Ladakh, you know. To a monastery. I hope   it   isn't   forever…"

"Why? What happened?"

"Why did you say that? Do you think something must've *happened* to prompt a decision like that?"

"Yes. Knowing him. Knowing anyone. Yes."

"I think it is that bloody girl again. He hasn't been the same after this one. He had committed himself too completely and too deeply and I think it just messed him up."

"She was not even pretty…"

"Yep. But I thought her hot, thin and fair and tall and all…nice clothes…worked on her hair…"

"They all work on their hair except us, Mee!"

– we're giggling with the superficial glee of the guilty jealous. –

"Boss, just make sure there are no bugs and all in my house."

"Please   trust   me!"

"Fine. No more of that."

"What did you want me to do for you?"

"Yah. That. I wanted you to buy me a small bottle, a quarter, of gin."

"You're not serious, Meera."

"I am, Deb."

"You don't want bugs but you want a drink?"

"I don't see how the two are comparable. Just one drink…I know how this looks but I feel this total high, I feel good…I just need a drink. That's all."

"Dude! You are not *supposed* to drink. Have you been doing this often?"

"That is where you come in. See, I cannot walk into a liquor shop without eliciting comments and thoughts such as the one that you just voiced. You need to go and get it for me."

"No! No way. I am not a party to this."

"Yes you are. Or you can forget about tonight."

– I don't like the way she is looking at me. She is supposed to be supportive and good and compliant. –

"Why don't you order it in at home?"

"Because they know that I am alone."

"Who? The liquor shop knows you're alone?"

"Don't be an ass. The guards know. And they will know what is in that supposedly discreet black polyethylene bag that the delivery boy will carry. And they will know that I am going to consume alcohol. Alone. And all. Won't look good."

"No. You're right. It doesn't look good at all. Even to me."

"You don't matter as much."

"Have you been drinking?"
"No. I haven't. I wouldn't be so desperate, would I?"

"Right. Just finish it before I come in. I will not see you do this, okay?"

"Wow! You are so bloody, Holier-Than-Thou now, aren't you...?"

"Sue me!"

They laugh, banishing the discomfort that was creeping up on them.

"You know, I messed with a cabby today. Do you remember I used to say that we should try this trick on them when they refused us a ride?"

"I don't believe you! You, what? Told him you want to go really far and got off midway?"

"Yep."

"You weren't scared?"

"No."

"They could be dangerous, Meera."

"Maybe. But I had to try it out. And it works. If you ever do it, make sure you can run away really fast or disappear into a building or something. Also, your face should be something he cannot remember you by."

"You are mad, you know that?"

"Mad? Why mad?"

"I mean to think of it is one thing. To do it is another. You could get killed for this type of nonsense."

"Not in Maharashtra. They would just bash the cabbie up."

"Bombay."

"Bombay, Maharashtra."

"You love this place, don't you?"

"No. I hate it. But I have faith in the people. You sound like my mother. She says the same things when she hears of my fighting and doing innovative stuff like my awesome cab ride today."

"You should be careful. Life is not for throwing away."

"And are you sure about that?"

"Aren't you?"

"I am. I'm sure. But sometimes you just do what you do."
"No you don't."

"Is that how your young life has learnt to live, Debbie? Making sacrifices?"

"I prioritize things. And my safety is priority."

"Hmmm. Have you met any men?"

"Yes, I have. But then I find that they are all boys. And I wish that I could be lesbian!" she laughs.

"You wish? I could totally be lesbian. I mean, in another life. I sometimes think of all of us women, living our lives…all the girls that I knew and loved settling down together. In one house. Bringing the sea of our experiences back into the cocoon that we came from. A sort of return to innocence. We will have the same pyjama parties, cut ice cream for birthdays, live frugally, then blow up our savings for the month in a night, and wake up the next morning and nurse each other's hangovers…"

– she is really laughing. She is pretty. Someone will find her and make her a very satisfied woman…then again she doesn't need that to be happy. She will be happy anyway. That is my blessing. Not that she is found by someone and made happy…that she is happy, content…anyway…found or not. –

"Yes! You will still be mad and defy your age. Completely immature and then, when no one expects it, you will speak like a very old woman…it will be your idea to go to Leo's and then we will all dress up and worry about the expense but you would have surprised us with some crazy plan you devised to save the money…"

"I know…but my plans were not crazy."

"Like when you threw out the cleaning woman and made us sweep and mop in turns for a month and then took us to a movie with the money that we had saved."

"And popcorn. The money paid for that, too! But we won't go to Leo's anymore. We will retire to a smaller town, Pune maybe and then find a small, quaint hangout for ourselves there."

"You don't like Leo's anymore?"
"Not since we went last. I don't like the way it's been taken over by the *kallu bhais*. Their dancing is sick…'

Thin men, delicious women
Dark, black
Swaying, no gyrating,
Grinding
Rolling
Up, up, up
Stop
Down, down, down
You wonder how they
Keep their balance
Savage moves that I don't understand
Each body is lost in itself
So focused on looking at themselves…
Heads bent, looking down, at the lowest moving parts of their bodies
Making those moves
And then
They eye a body part of the other, moving like their own…
And they bring themselves in asymmetrical sync for sometime
Till they hear the same beat beating again
In their own different ways…
They hold their lower jaws out,
lips parted, contorted faces
engrossed in the trying intensity of that dance form,
eliciting creepy passion, which must match the intensity of their moves…
They look like they want to do it right there…
Completely sexed up…
Sway, gyrate, grind, up and down…
I don't understand it
No eye contact except when it is over
And even then
So fleeting

Like professional sex or something…
And those mirrors…such a distraction
Havens for the club goers' perverse dancing with
themselves…
And because they thrust and shake with such precision
Sincerely watching their own every move
I want to burst out laughing

Because that sexed up gaze, that jutting jaw and purposefully
pursed mouth
In the world, which the door of this dimly lit club shuts out
is a constipated person trying real hard
I don't want to laugh when I am drinking to be able to dance
When I am drinking to be able to cry…I need that gin and
tonic

"No place is the same without us being us. I miss you,
you know? I miss all of us. And I am really looking
forward to the time that I am going to spend at your
place!"

– that has been worrying me for some time. How will I
manage with this intrusion? Shall I tell her that we will
mind our own businesses?

No. Just take it as it comes. Manage it then. –

"Yep. Shall we split?"

"Yes! I better go organize my things. I will carry some books. I will have to study. So I hope you are not planning a party!"

"I am not planning a party. I will let you be. Now, I will wait outside the shop while you go in and get it. I take Blue Riband."

"That is one of the cheapest ones, isn't it? You are not earning just ten thousand Rupees now! Take a better brand."

"I am not sure they all supply a quarter... try Bombay Sapphire, then. If he doesn't have a quarter, get a half. I will have to figure how to dispose of it. Garbage from a house tells you a story, you know?"

"Yes it does!" agrees Debbie with wasted sarcasm.

– making love to his tonic and gin...

He says, 'Son can you play me a memory
I'm not really sure how it goes
But   it's   sad   and   it's   sweet
And   I   knew   it   complete
When I wore a younger man's clothes...

La La la la... di da da dum

Sing   us   a   song   you're   the   piano   man
Sing us a song tonight

We love that song. We had thought that we liked whiskey, till we heard the song together…

Kept rewinding to this part…
'making love to his tonic and gin…'

As if, by rewinding, we'd hear more than we did the first time, and time and again.

Was there something we were looking for? Was it the heavy sound of the piano… did it not sound like a carnival?

What were we looking for?

Yes, they're sharing a drink they call loneliness
But it's better than drinking alone…

What were we sharing? The words…? Words that rang a bell? Made you crave for…Tonic and gin…? –

"Here's your Sapphire. Where are you off to now?"

"Here and there. May go home for a bit. I feel a little tired."
"You should rest. You're not planning to drink right away, are you?"

"God! Leave me alone, woman! No. I'm not. Okay? Now, bye."

– quick hug. We'll meet soon enough.

Hail that cab.

He stopped. –

"Colaba *jana hai*?"

– he's agreed.

Let's go!

Home. Want to go home now.

Walked too long. Throbbing in my legs.

I feel the blood dizzily running around trying to comfort the aching muscles that are calling to it. The blood rushes everywhere, embracing each screaming muscle and silencing its agony. It bursts through my veins in spurts and waves. If I looked at my naked legs just now, I would be able to see the pulsating, blood flowing, taking its course abounding narrow gorges, flooding them...

I will not sleep. Won't waste the day. I like this cab. Not that Fiat type. Spacious van. Will not hit my head on its filthy roof each time it goes over the potholes and breakers.

What will I do? Maybe I *will* sleep. To a fairy tale…

Which way shall he drive us, he is asking?

He allows me a great freedom…the freedom of choice…
–

"Marine Drive *se nikaal leejiye*."

– may as well have a look at the sea. Reconfirm my apprehensions…

I am going to sing! A good song…lovely song…in my head, of course.
I believe in wonders…
Something good in everything I see…

Hmmm hmmm…a dream…a fantasy…
To help me through…reality…

My escape.

My fairy tale.

I believe in wonders…la la la la la la la la…
I have a dream…hmmm hmmm hm hmmm

Do I?

I do.

How can you not believe in wonders? ABBA. Lovely ABBA of my childhood.

Ah! The sea…the Indian Ocean…the Arabian Sea…but wait…

It looks as forlorn as ever…no colour in its cheeks…

I was right, it stinks… –

*   *   *

– walking home now.

 My legs feel better but I will sleep…

To a story…a fairy tale.
I can hear the opening credits of *my* fairy tale.

Yes! This is what I will do!

Why was I confused?

Thank you for the music, Carl Davis…

The soundtrack plays in my head now. Some days, it is in my head all day.

Makes my mind dance.

To a tune no one else hears.

Darcy…and the soft notes from *Thinking About Lizzy*…

A single man of large fortune…must be in want of a wife

And how Jennifer Ehle says it…

I'm tired. Should not fight it.

But sleep fights me…constantly.

I will counter that with *Pride and Prejudice*. I'm home. No man compares with Colin Firth – the master of subtlety.

I run into his arms the way Eliza Bennett never will.
In the English countryside…
He holds me…
Darcy…!

Where is the DVD, now?

Here!

Trembling hands and the DVD player…

The English countryside of the BBC's *Pride and Prejudice*…and the main cast on the cover!

I know this sound.

The DVD player whirrs to life accepting my offering.

No glitches. No unrecognized formats and file types.

I will watch this movie. It will make me sleep. I know.

4:15 P.M. –

*   *   *

– oh no! Not the phone. Hope it isn't the office!

It's AJ. –

"Hi! Again."

"Good time, Mee?"

"Always is, darling!"

"You haven't had enough of me?"

"Never!"

"So I am packing a light bag and I thought about what you want from there? And then I realized that I may not be near shops."

"Good. Always good when you call. Are you already feeling one with the Universe?"

"Sort of. You know, I have no plans, no ambition. I just want to get on the flight. Want to pack my bag. I want enough warm clothes. I don't want more."

"Hmmm. You are like your fish, remember? When you connected with that goldfish in a bowl?"

"Yes, I remember. She was telling me something…"

"She planted a pouty kiss on the bowl. I loved the way that you put it. And she had swum smiling to you. That was poetic."

"Yes. I think that she was telling me that the bowl was enough because that is what I was wondering without really knowing it. I think that is the time that you are best situated to receive a message. And you need to trust the message."

"Yes. But if I remember correctly, you saw two fish in the bowl. You were not wondering about the bowl being enough but in fact about the two of them being together in the bowl being enough. Weren't you?"

"I think so. My God! What a memory!"

"My memory is crap, as you are well aware. It was the whole thing and how you described it."

"Yah. Anyone else would have laughed! You didn't."

"That was because I believed you. I have experienced it myself, you know. I connected with my kitten, Zorro. She just loved me. There was a lunar eclipse that I had decided to stay awake for. Naturally, she gave me unquestioning company through the late night, dozing on the voluminous text book on Administrative Law. When I moved out of the house for the eclipse, she stretched and followed me into the moonlight. I stared up at the moon, and I got this feeling when the eclipse started. I looked down at my feet and saw the kitten staring up, past me at the eclipsed moon. And then, our eyes met in a look that can only pass between humans, appreciating the same thing. Humans. Equals. Not one human and one animal. Now, focus on this one, AJ."

"I am focusing."

"Can you imagine, looking down the length of your body at the cat sitting at your feet? You are wearing pyjamas. The thick hosiery variety. And you think, at that instant, that your leg looks like the trunk of a tree. And at that exact moment, you look again at the cat that you were sharing the eclipse with and she starts to climb your leg. Hurting you. But you forget to cry out in pain because you are struck with how the two of you were thinking the exact same thing. That my leg was the trunk of a tree, like the Asoka tree that she would climb and scratch her claws on every day. And that is exactly what she set out to do on mine!"

"You did eventually kick her away, I hope?"

"I pulled her away and yelled at her to stop scratching me and she was apologetic, you know? So human about that too."

"Or you were so…feline?"

"Maybe. Like you were…you were piscine about that amazing woman who you thought you loved."

"I didn't mean it like that."

"Just the tone. You are discounting my experience with a cat when you were taken seriously about a fish."

"I am sorry. It's just the bit about equals that I found funny. I mean did you equal the cat or did the cat equal you, you know? Hey! Just one of our jokes. I am sorry. Don't misunderstand me, please! Please!"

"I can do funny too. You thought that the fish bowl was enough, didn't you? What do you expect when you talk with goldfish, AJ? Today, you are hoping that running away to Ladakh is enough because you are probably connecting with a monk on Orkut or wherever it is that you wander. Let's forget it, okay? Why did you call?"

"I wanted to ask you something."

"I cannot marry you…!"

They laugh.
"No. I won't put you in a spot about that…don't worry."

They laugh some more…

"You know. Did I tell you about this guy who I thought would ask me to marry him?"

"No. He did not ask you, then?"
"Listen. He was the passionate sort. And well, he was romantic and as a girl, you like that kind of thing, you know? He never laughed at certain jokes and how he remained a gentleman even when all the other guys lost their heads and stuff."

"You do know that such a guy is a total fake, right?"

"That isn't the point. So well, one day this guy, let's call him Jim, comes over to nonchalant, old me and he is with this other guy who is also a sort-of-friend…and this sort-of-friend guy says that Jim wants to speak with me…alone. So I say yes and jump off my perch to take a walk with Jim. I was a little surprised that Jim approached me like that because Jim and I were close pals at the time. This fact set off warning bells in the old head. So we walked up the avenue to the classrooms, and he said that he had wanted to ask me this for a long time and that he could not sleep at night anymore and that he was going mad. I told him to just stop!"

"You didn't want him?"

"I don't know. It is just the first thing you say in such situations, don't you?"

"Do you? Because that means you are liars, man! I mean, a guy asks and then you first vehemently ask him to stop and now, you're telling me that all the times that I stopped, as requested, I stood a chance?"

"This is my story, AJ. Not yours. Don't mix it up with your loser life. You should have asked more than once, anyway. And why the hell do you chaps spring surprises like the aforesaid Jim? Why can you not just write…or just calmly say something like, I am a good guy…will you like to get to know me better? I do want to get to know you better, and I mean more than as friends…or something? No, correction. Don't say the 'more than as friends' piece. We run away from that, too."

"How would writing help?"

"Immediate reactions, idiot! You are not in front of me for me to ask you to stop… gives me a chance to mull over the proposal instead of doing what one usually does, that being, ask you to stop…now shut up and listen to what happened. Also, writing's old fashioned and we like that."

"Why can you not just say that you will think about it when we speak with you? Who says that you have to answer then? Like right then?"

"You make it sound like a business proposition. All logical and reasonable. Big mistake. Maybe we know that you put us on a pedestal when you ask and maybe we like sitting on said pedestal for as long as we bloody like. Don't you see? I say 'yes', you say 'whoops!' and it's over. We are equals. Too soon. You say, 'Please!' I say, 'No!' I still sit up there and I may even be something that you will never get! Now, can I get back to what I was talking about?"

"Fine. Tell me."

"Where was I?"

"You asked the sod to stop."

"He was surprised when I asked him to stop. And he asked me if I knew already. I said, that only an idiot would not have guessed. Jim then asked me whether he stood a chance. And I said no, he didn't. And then he started to bloody cry. Hey! I said. Dude...this is not about you. And then, AJ, and you have to hear this carefully, he said those words...and I will tell you, my friend, that I am so grateful that he said those horrid words before I had said the next thing on my mind...those horrid, horrid, words...you there, AJ?"

"I am. And all ears...those words were..."

"He said, 'Not about me? Then is it about her? What about her?' Her!"

"Her?"

"*Her*. AJ, *her*! I realized that I had blundered. He was asking for my advice about a female friend, obviously, and at that exact moment, I guessed who that might be and *knew* that it wasn't me, of course."

"Did you tell him?"

"Are you mad? I stayed with the general trend of the conversation and explained to him why it wouldn't work out."

"Why didn't you clear it up?"

"Clear it up? Meaning, tell him that I had mistakenly thought that he was in love with me? Are you mad?"

"You would've laughed about it, like friends! He wouldn't have minded at all. He would not even have mentioned it...ever!"

"No way! Too embarrassing. It was bad enough that he hadn't chosen me above all women. All men should, no? And to tell him that I thought he had meant me and not *her* after the emotional manner and the sheer finality with which I had asked him to stop and said, no! No way. That would have been too much."

"Vanity. Vanity. You are vain. That's it."
"Maybe I am. In any case, it is quite generally established that I was much better than *her*. Everyone, at the end of Law School infinitely preferred me to her. *Capisce*?"

"And he took it. He should never have trusted you."

"I agree. You should trust no one. I don't trust me…"

"He believed you and did not investigate this separately?"

"Yes. I let him believe that I had seen through his ill-masked feelings for her."

"Poor sod! What a sucker!"

"You insult me. He wasn't a sucker. He is a partner in one of India's leading law firms and we are completely out of touch. She was just not for him and he wasn't for her. There's no two ways about it."

"He could've tried!"
"Or were they meant for each other, they would've happened!"

"Had you not interfered…Yes!"

"I didn't interfere, circumstances did. In fact, I don't know why he didn't go to her directly. Must've been a deeper than usual crush. Such an awe-inspired demeanor towards the opposite party is a recipe for things not working out. Period."

"Awe-inspired? How else do you respect and love the person?"

"Oh you do! But for how long can you remain in awe of someone who you will hear fart one day? What then?

What next? You fall hard and that is why it does not work. I am sorry to say this but look at you! How many times have you fallen so deeply in love that you crush your very being to become the person that those girls want you to be? And how hard it hurts when they are done with you!"

"Yes it hurts but I do not lose awe of them. They are still the great women I thought they were."
"They ditched you, AJ! They took you for granted and fooled you. They cannot therefore be great! Did you hear them fart? Be honest."

"How can you even speak like this?"

"You did. That means that you did. And you remained in awe of them? AJ, wake up. You can only be 'great' as party to a relationship if you are not human. There is no greatness between husband and wife and girlfriend and boyfriend, brother and sister, parent and child, at least not the larger-than-life picture that you tend to paint of the whole damn charade!"

"And you really believe in destiny? And that things are meant to be and that one doesn't have to make things happen?"

"Yes. But, we will be cautious. You must ask me why I believe in destiny. And you must also know that there are no absolutes. It isn't that I advise you to sit before a speeding car instead of jumping out of its way, okay? The usual disclaimers."

"Why do you believe in destiny?"
"Because I believe in parallel lives."

"What are those?"

"It is a thought that is just taking form. I believe that life is too short and that some of us hardly live it, some die in accidents, some get blown up by terrorists, some are orphaned, some are lucky, some do what they wanted to always do, some slog it out at a desk that they know was never meant for them, some are rich, too many poor…all these things that just don't make sense. There has to be some hope! And hope demands that all of us, each of us, get what we want. Like in fairy tales, but not just in the end because there are no ends and no beginnings. Simultaneousness defines the phenomenon. In another life, Jim and 'her' did happen. In a parallel life, they broke up two years later, in another parallel life, they lived happily ever after…etcetera, etcetera. Follow the drift?"

"Yes…yes, yes I do. So in another life, I am…I am not as unlucky as I am in love."

"Yes. You are Don Juan!"

"I don't want to be Don Juan."

"Romeo?"

"No!"

"Well...okay, you are with the last lady that ditched you, hitched firmly by your side in matrimony and all that. Don't laugh."

"You are absolutely screwed up, my friend! Even more than I am! Now I know why you aren't going to a monastery in Ladakh and why I am! You have run away from reality. You have so run away! If and only if this wasn't one of your silly postulates that are very entertaining when you intend it! If you were serious about what you have been saying these last few minutes, you are lost."

"I am serious, AJ. Go to the monastery if you have to but know this, the sorrow that is troubling you today, is happiness in another world. It has to be. It makes no sense that kids are killed during conflicts – is there a greater grief you can imagine than the one that living parents of a dead child go through? It makes no sense that you are going to work one day and get killed in a bomb blast - never to return, get hacked in a civil war that you were not fighting, fall prey to a leopard in place of your goat, get raped and murdered on your way to school, get your skull broken by a sledgehammer just when escaping a war-ravaged town and die looking into the dead eyes of the person who got hit before you, your heads on stones, side-by-side, flat on the ground...part of a mass grave...so that your remains are found years later and it does not matter who you were. It makes no sense that you die in a plane crash. All untimely deaths that cannot have been intended. They break the circle of life. And it is not consoling to believe that God works in mysterious ways. There has to be more. Forget hope. Don't give me hope…give me the full circle. Where our beginnings are the same, we are all born the same way or thereabouts, why should the ends be different? We are all created in the same way, through the same mechanics, even if we live different lives, are different people, why should our deaths be various? The variety in our lives is dramatic enough. Thank you very bloody much!"

"This how you explain life?"
"I am beginning to. And I have never felt such complete clarity. It all falls into place. It answers all the questions. I am a famous writer. Wherever I go, people ask me to sign my books and tell me how much they love my work."

"Shut up. Just stop now. You won't write?"

"That is not the point, AJ! I don't write, anyway. Don't you get it? I should. But I don't. And we could never explain this in all our discussions. How could I forget 'Making a Sacrifice'? Why do I stick with a job that I no longer enjoy when apparently, I know what I seem to want? We never understood why I don't try harder. But now *I* understand."

"You know, the first step in spiritual life is the darkness of the soul. Stop doubting, don't look so much into the future, don't look back, just do what you should be doing. Don't stop. Don't worry about the consequences, the fruit of your labour. You can control only your own actions. Shoot the arrow, it will find its mark. We always had the answers to the questions that you have listed. You forgot about 'Making a Sacrifice' because that is just not the right place for you to publish. I don't know why, but they will not publish your work. I think it is because I would never read those journals. Who does? It was easy to forget. You stick to your job for the usual reason – the money helps. You have a loan to pay off. And the time that you steal to write is the least of your struggles, your metamorphosis, if you will. You want it all enough to castigate yourself each time you cannot be true to your job and your passion, which just happen to be different things. We always had the answers."

"Anyway, look where we've come with this whole thing, AJ. You said you wanted to ask me something…"

"I wanted to ask you whether you really thought I was running away when I told you that I was off to Ladakh when we spoke this morning."

– I don't know what to say. He hears the silence. We both do. –

"I'm going to hang up now."

"Yah. I was watching a movie. It is still running."

"Bye."

"Yep."

CHAPTER 4
EVENING

– I am like Al Pacino in *Insomnia*. I didn't kill anyone, though. Not yet.

I just can't sleep when the sun is still out.

Darken the room.

Focus on *Pride & Prejudice*.

Fast forward to the dance at Netherfield but first, watch Lizzy and Darcy meet when she walks in the slush to meet Jane. I love Colin Firth. He is the master of subtlety.

And then, that conversation! Cut out the Lizzy-Jane dialogue on 'my Mr. Bingley' and jump to this...

I have faults enough but they are not, I hope, of understanding...

My good opinion once lost, is lost forever.

Resentful alright, Darcy!

You will regret this!

That is a failing indeed, but I cannot laugh at it…

You will laugh, Lizzy. Just like you will dance with him after having safely promised *'never to dance with Mr. Darcy'*…!

Best scenes. Best moments…

*   *   *

The curtains in this room don't meet in perfect symmetry.

Still a ray of the strong evening sun creeping in. It plays on the rotating arms of the ceiling fan.

An illusion.

Two versions of these beams. One, on the fan's rotating arms. Rotating *blades*, not arms. And one, the other, past the blades, on the ceiling. But they are really the same single beam that is irritating me.

Pull the cushions closer. The beams dance with the fan.

I don't really care for the dance that they dance…Lizzy and Mr. D. don't like the music. And there is this bit of conversation that I just don't get. I should Google for it. Can't remember it from the book.

Mary Bennet sings a terrible song at the dance at Netherfield Park.

Lower volume.

Sleepy.

So we argued…AJ and I. He is pissed, I guess. I will have to call him later. He won't call me. He is hurt.

But it had to be done. His bubble had to burst. His mourning has no end! You have to be honest with friends.

Lydia's misbehaving at the Ball at Netherfield. Mrs. Bennet, you sound like a fool. Good acting, Alison Steadman…

I am smiling…in my sleep…yes, yes, I know these scenes –

the rotating beam on the fan blades
pulls me up to it
into the rotating blades of the ceiling fan
with a centripetal force
till I realize that the blades will slice me
like a cucumber…

pulling me in faster

strengthening force
I'm in the fan…
and past it

not a scratch
he is waiting for me
Hemant Bhai

he's crying, sitting at the table with a plate of…of sliced cucumbers…?
His wife is dead…she hung herself from the ceiling fan…I can see her now… top view…her head seems to carry the weight of the body…

he lunges at me

I look at the ceiling fan below me
shall I jump?

he wants to kill me

we're in the sunny English countryside

'why did you do it?

Why did you steal my story?

I trusted you…!

do you know what she did! She killed herself…' his sobbing leaves him weak…

My voice, 'why did she do it?'

'You think you can call her 'Mrs. S' and she would not know!
You used my daughter's pet name...you killed her, you sorry
writer...
Can't make an original? I will kill you...'

why can't I run?

Music...I hear music...?
I cannot dance...why the music?

My voice is singing now, 'I'll delete that story, okay? Won't
submit it for the competition...
I'll make a sacrifice...let me go! I'm so sorry...!'

She's woken from the dead...
rising towards me from the fan, which rotates under me...
past my feet...
her head hangs unnaturally on the side...

her ghost is crying...'how did you know so much?'

'I...I imagined it...so sorry...' My voice sings to the
music...where is it coming from...?
'Hemant Bhai mentioned it all in passing...no details...I
swear!
Don't kill me...it won't be published, okay? I promise...No
one will publish it...
I gave it the details – they were mine, my imagination, my
articulation, my...my foolishness, my genius, my...'

menacing wail...she turns to her husband 'you didn't tell her all that...?'

'No! No!' he weeps

I'm crying too...so sorry...we're all crying...where is Tuk, though?
Hemant's killed in a sweep...

smiles at me...'I'm taking him with me...I should have asked, I just felt so betrayed...so naked...shouldn't have acted on impulse...but it will be alright now...we're together again...'

wait! What about Tuk?

'oh! I took her already...I wouldn't leave her alone...'

they're gone...like that
Because I wrote that story about what happened on Tuk's birthday...

– awake.

Sweating.

Closing credits. The BBC's *Pride & Prejudice*.

'Soundtrack by Carl Davis' flashes on the TV.

That's where the music came from.

I can't write an original. Forget good or bad, I can't *even* write an original. –

*   *   *

Did I go back to sleep?

5 P.M.

I did. Deep one, too.

Horrid dream. Stale taste in my mouth. I should get up.

Wait!
Someone is in the house.
I am tired of this violation!
I am not scared.

I am as watchful and alert as a commando. I am superhuman.
I can fly…when I want to. When I really, really, need to.

Someone is in the other room.
I am alert. How can I catch him? Surprise him? The element
of surprise.
The importance of being Frank…Hardy.
What would Frank Hardy do? He would wait. Wait for this
person to make a move. Wait. Wait.
I see a reflection in the vase.
A convoluted reflection in the convex vase on the sideboard.
he sees me, too…we see each other…

No need to hide now

I am flying…across the room…at the vase…I will catch you!
The reflection, too…is flying…she sees me…I see her…
the reflection is a bird… it is …

It is real…it is…
I hover around the vase…I have wings that flutter…
The reflection is ME
I AM FALLING…FALLING…

WAKE UP!

I scream in my head.

Someone strokes my hair.

My heart has stopped.

What the …

The ghost again…who is it?
Cold.

I am cold. I am lying with my head in his or her lap.

When did this happen?

Who? What?

Is this?

A whisper, *don't worry. Don't be sacred. I will not harm you. It's just me. Look up, Meera. Don't be afraid.*

I push my heavy body up with my arms, hands flat on the floor. I want to run but I are heavy, too heavy and too slow.

I look up.

A woman. In white. Smiling. Kind eyes. But that makes no damn difference. She is either a ghost or an illusion. And that means I'm dead, going to be dead or just plain crazy. Plain crazy, dead…same difference.

You are not dead. You are only as crazy as everyone else. You are as crazy as the person who last wished they never grew up. As crazy as the guy who lied and liked it when he did. Let me hold your hands to make them warm.
I want to pull my hands away. Do I have a choice?

Yes you do, Meera.

She doesn't move.

I speak for the first time after seeing her. "You can read my thoughts?"

No. I can hear them. So it doesn't matter whether you put them in inverted commas or not.

That is a relaxation, indeed! Who are you?

I am you.

You don't look like me. You look…you look like…hey! Elizabeth Bennett.

Not like Jennifer Ehle?

No. Not like her. Just dressed like Lizzy Bennet, I guess? Which is strange because I see Elizabeth Bennett as Jennifer Ehle, she was so much better than all of those actresses who aspired to be her. So you should look like her. But you don't. This is very, very strange.

I can look like whoever you want me to. I can be Alice, Goldilocks, the Little Match Girl, Thumbelina, or even Tweedledum and Tweedledee.
The Famous Five?

Yes. Do you want me to show you?

No. Sorry. I think I was joking. Cracking up a little, you know? Should I be screaming for help?

You needn't be afraid, I have told you. Besides, as you mentioned this morning, the residents of this neighbourhood would hardly respond to your screaming. Just like they don't respond to that car alarm that goes off every morning.

Wait! I did not '*mention*' this. I thought it. And I was alone. Except that I felt a presence at about that time…in the shower.

She smiles.

The presence wasn't me. But I have heard you, shared your memories and your dreams, or sometimes, your nightmares. I know you! I know that you've always had a secret crush on Frank Hardy and he is still the man in your dreams.

You've been around all day?

I've been around these twenty-seven years and nine months and some days. I've been with you all the time. I watch you, I speak to you, and we see things together and have even exchanged glances, I walk around the room or sit opposite you and between us we observe so many, many things. Do you have no recollection? Haven't you felt that you were on both sides of the table, watching everyone including yourself during meetings, in drawing rooms, in shops and all the other places?

No. You cannot be God, if you are me. Are you an angel?

I am anything you believe me to be. I know you.

I used to think that I'd have a special friend when I was a kid. Someone who'd write my exam for me. Invisible to all except me.

I am that friend. I am real. No childhood fantasy.

No. You aren't. This is the first time I've seen you. And I wrote my own exams.

We did together! You haven't seen me because you've been blind! But now I am here. To stay. When you need me, I will be there...just like I have been there all these years...but tangibly now. I am your one true friend.

And if I don't want you?

You will always need me. Everyone needs a friend. I only respond to your subconscious.

That is convenient. So when you impose yourself uninvited, I just have to believe that bullshit. I cannot confirm with my subconscious, can I?

Let's try it.

Gone! She's gone...

I should brush my teeth and get the hell out of here! I need to brush. I will be sick.

*   *   *

– she said 'tangibly now'...why now?

Because now is as good a time as any other. You know this. Can we not get past the unnecessary denial and come to the point?

I know that she is in the mirror. I know that while I look down at the gaping washbasin, my reflection stares at me as if …

As if it was accusing you of denial!

I look up.

I see her.

I see me.
Now is as good a time as any other. I know this. Can we not get past the unnecessary denial and come to the point?

What is the point?

There is none.

Not anymore. That is why you like short stories.

I wish that I had written enough short stories to be able to make that claim with any credibility. Or in fact, even *read* enough…!
And that is the point. When is enough? Why and how is enough?

I know. When and how is enough? When and how do you know that you have the best, or the worst? You know, I cannot list my favourite books and I have always been cryptic and mysterious about the answer to that question…till I heard many others say the very same thing that I always thought: there cannot be *favourites*. It is, once you think about it, a very stupid question! Favourite *author*? Favourite ice cream flavour, I understand. Author. I don't.

Today, you like short stories, though.

Yes. I do. I mean you could like an O'Henry as much as an Agatha Christie, I guess. You know, I judge my favourite books by the standard of whether *I* would like to have written them. It is a pretty passable standard, I am easy to impress and I wish that I had been born before most of the authors I have read to have been able to pre-empt their work.

I will not ask you which ones are your favourites.

Yes. Don't.

Which would you have written first?

Oh! I don't know. Different ones at different times. One of the truest forms of telling a story is one where the thoughts or the state of mind of the protagonist is reported directly. It isn't easy to be true to any form of storytelling without an understanding and cooperative reader. I mean, *The Catcher in the Rye* is about a boy recollecting four or five or a few or whatever days of his life. Do you really recollect days of your life like that? I mean, do you remember *exactly* what you thought at a certain time in every one of the hours of the past couple of days in sequence and then the actions – your own and everyone else's?

Ackley's pimples are unforgettable, of course but it goes on and on during the moments that he is recollecting – all in order of occurrence. He remembers and restates precise conversations, man! So Ackley has pimples and is always bursting them, has no hanky. But, that Ackley walks about the room, picks up Sally's picture, discusses and expresses shock over the fencing match that did not happen...and every movement, every action, every word...reported...recollected...like a record playing in sequence. Not garbled, confused or mixed up. It all appears disjointed...but it is really linear. Unbelievably, linear.

You are not an understanding and cooperative reader?

I am not easily fooled. The fact that Ackley picked up Stradlater's knee support off Stradlater's chiffonier and therefore chucked it on Stradlater's bed and the sheer length of their entire conversation...God!

Then, enter, Stradlater. Holden's doing a tap dance to entertain him, then that he is out of breath and takes off his hat and looks at it for the nineteenth time.

Who remembers taking off a hat?

For the nineteenth time? Unless your scalp comes off with it, why would you remember that? And that you looked at it? Such detailed, photographic memory. Frame by frame…of the few days that he is recounting? Right!

I liked the book. I did. I do. But I don't like being manipulated. I don't like clever devices.

He remembers everything from start to finish! Everything. In the order that it happened. Then, to lend a tone of reality to the whole thing, he forgets how much money he had when he gets out of the hotel where Maurice or someone, the pimp, bashes him. It is all synthetic, you know…he doesn't remember this or that but generally has a bloody sharp memory…perfectly linear recollection of every detail. I don't understand it. He recollects what Sally wears, every line of conversation. Why did he have to remember it then? JD could've just told us the story directly.

Look what I came across…another specimen.

Hmmm…The Handmaid's Tale?

Yes. It was right here. I don't know where it could have gone. I left the book on this table. Right here.

Yes, but then you were cleaning the bookshelf on Sunday and put it where it belongs.

Shock.

I turn to her.

She sits on the sofa staring smilingly back at me, asking me...

Why are you surprised?

Yes. I shouldn't be, should I? It will take getting used to.

You want me to get it out? I remember where you put it.

Yes, please.

Still shocked. I watch her move to the bookshelf and reach for the red and white book by Margaret Atwood.

She hands it to me and seats herself at the dining table, chin cupped in hand, leaning on a single elbow. She cannot be comfortable for long unless she also puts her left arm on the table...which she now has done. She is ready. For what?

I thought you were going to read to me...
Not really. Just wanted to show you something. A page that I had dog-eared.

Yes.

See this? I move to the table and sit next to her.

See, she writes, '*I would like to believe this is a story I am telling…*'

Ta ta ta ta ta…it goes on. Then she writes, '*It isn't a story I am telling. It's also a story I am telling in my head, as I go along… But if it's a story, even in my head, I must be telling it to someone. You don't tell a story only to yourself. There's always someone else.*'

Etcetera etcetera.

Then she says, '*A story is like a letter. Dear You, I'll say…*' And on and on.

She seems to have wanted to bring to an idiot reader's notice that this was the stream of consciousness method she was using…and then, in the end, there is an entire Chapter titled 'HISTORICAL NOTES ON *The Handmaid's Tale*' which begins by stating that this is a transcript of some symposium on the made-up country to which her protagonist had belonged. And the transcript involves intellectuals dissecting the facts surrounding 'The Handmaid's Tale', which was discovered on a tape or something many years after the Handmaid had lived and probably died.

The point is this. The Historical Notes chapter doesn't really add to the substance of the story. I mean *1984* ends as it does. You don't find the author overanalyzing his story with a conference of intellectuals meeting in the world after fifty or a hundred years and then discussing the events.

1984 has an epilogue. On Newspeak.

Yes, yes! But it does not try to explain the author's approach to how he told the story. That epilogue is like Tolkien explaining to you the fundamentals of Elvish. Orwell is not trying to tell you why he wrote what he wrote or why he wrote it like he did. You can say that his epilogue suggests that 1984 is a thing of the past and all of that but he is not worried that you just didn't get it. Whereas in *The Handmaid's Tale*, that Ofred was telling you her story, that you were in her head, is not something that the author felt the reader would comprehend, or something. So she wrote a whole chapter to suggest that the story that we had witnessed was actually a voice recording from Ofred's memory, which was being heard by or read by historians or something many years later...Again, Ofred's story is linear. Over a longer period of time but always in order of occurrence. How could she remember it like that? How could she remember like that particularly given the events of the story and the general state of mind of all the characters?

Atwood should have stopped where she did.

She needn't have bothered explaining her plot and style of writing. The 'story' has thoughts, and dreams intermingling like they should but yes, over a course of some or many months...you must have a reader who is willing to play along and acknowledge that it makes little sense to list every waking hour of the day and every minute of the protagonist's thoughts for the span of time that the story covers. Atwood wasn't confident of our acceptance. What she was doing was telling the Handmaid's tale for the Handmaid. Only seemingly through the Handmaid because the author clearly picked which thoughts of each day she wanted us to know about. Why was Atwood so apologetic about the whole thing? That is the question.

Such stories must also be just the right length.

Yes. The right length means focusing on a single day, or two, at most. Or a series of incidents covering a longer period of time, that are truly relevant to the piece. Twenty four hours with the protagonist that give you a complete insight into his head, or not. Like in Mrs. Dalloway.

You could write an epic if you expanded the dates and generations that your story covers. Twenty four hours is nothing.

It's enough. If you like short stories.

*   *   *

You know, I am glad that you are here. And real.

I know.

There is so little time for conversation and discovery now…the mornings are not long…now that we have been working so many years and are out of touch with the friends with who we rode the highs and lows of long mornings and the never ending nights. The nights now end in eight hours of tired sleep. It is impossible for me to find people who have read the same books and authors as I have, people who watch the same movies...someone you can have a meaningful conversation with and no, I don't mean you have to agree with me. But a real conversation, not part of online forums or chat rooms where everyone has no time to read what everyone else is saying, where some people type faster than you and upload their nonsense with all those typos that put you off...You do know what I mean, don't you?

I do. I do. And I am glad that I am here. And real.

I did not like the way AJ reacted to my connecting with Zorro. I'm not feeling so bad about giving him a taste of his own medicine. The best do fall, don't they?

I am sure that he is sorry.

Yes, of course. He will be off soon and when he is back – I am sure that he will be back – we will meet like pals again. My beautiful baby cat, Zorro with her small white kitten face and the black panda circles around her eyes – her mask. Her green, green, grey eyes. Shrewd cat eyes. So innocent.

She was my little lamb, followed me everywhere. Even into the late night lunar eclipse.

Late nights were easy back then.

Yes. The night was a sea of possibilities. You could cram for an exam, read a novel, or think that you were writing poetry.

Hmmm. Cats are not invincible.

And how I learnt that! Her nine lives were up before she was a cat. We rushed her to the vet but he had not studied cats. He'd trained on dogs, he understood dogs. Not cats. He never admitted it, of course. I realized this much later after I had had time to think about it.

All the stuff in his clinic was doggy stuff, dog related. No felines. No cats stared out of supplement cartons. The only cats in his clinic were the ones featured in a Dogs & Cats calendar the pages of which were always turned to many months before. And even it had more dogs than cats. I should have researched doctors. You *have to know cats*, you know? And canaries and rabbits and turtles and all.

He picked her out of the carton that we had carried her in
Like her mother would have picked her – by the scruff of her neck
Her stretched skin pulled back the loose skin from her kitten body
And her eyes shone! Deep emerald green…

I shout – in my head – she's alive! Can't you see? Her eyes are
shining! Cat green!
The same green that the eclipsed moon had shone in…
The shouting stays in my head.

I know she had died sometime back when I had smelt the
hairball
she had vomited
Long before we got to the Vet…

This is life. You know that.

I wish that there were potions for life forever…I wish
that there were no goodbyes, not permanent ones, at
least. I wish that there was permanent status quo.

What can you do? How can you resist resilient truth? Is it not
best to bow down, to embrace it? To love your life for the
moment and give it up when you have to?
But it isn't my life and living that bothers me. I would
like to go first, you know? So that I don't have to be the
one who gets left behind. Don't you just love that line in
Iris?

I'd give up forever to touch you
'Cause I know that you'll feel me somehow…

Tra… laa… laa, laa, la… laa la la laa la

When everything feels like the movies

You bleed just to know you're alive…

And the gruffness with which he sings the lines. They play in my head a lot, these lines. And as usual, I don't know the complete song. The Goo Goo Dolls', *Iris*.

It is all a movie, isn't it? The drama of our lives.

Yes. And you'll bleed just to know you're alive. What then? Should you be alive? Or is it time to let go? What if there is no drama? What if it is a boring movie?

Let go of what?

Once you have bled to know that you're alive…what next? You don't retire to the woods for salvation anymore. It is a balding forest and you will probably be evicted by a mining company and its saws and diggers. Your comfortable cave would be a gateway to some type of ore or the other and they'd want you to move.

The one path to salvation is therefore, to die.

You don't just die when you want to.

Are you throwing me a challenge? I can say it.

Say what?

That you *can* die when you want to.

Suicide?

Words that presuppose a state of mind. Words that judge. The state of thinking. Names that reek of disapproval. Assume motives. Names and words and phrases illustrating the intolerant thinking because of which there is no peace in this world.

A happy man kills himself?

Why not? You don't kill yourself. You jump off a balcony because you are so elated, you want it to stop. Just then. You want to move on, maybe. Why do we see it as an end? And an unhappy one at that? Isn't jumping off the balcony acceptance of the only or resilient truth?

What is acceptance? How does one define it? Explain *acceptance*? I'm saying don't wait for it to hit you. Strike first. Cheat this truth. Don't wait to embrace it. Give this truth or whatever it is a chance to embrace you.

You are not serious.

I am. But I will not be taken seriously. Not from the watching crowd that doesn't have it in it to accept *my truth*...biased with centuries of conditioning about life being too precious to take away, a crowd that takes its useless life so seriously, and waits to succumb to a cancer, or a bomb, or drunken drivers.

And maybe, ripe, pleasant, fulfilling old age.

Old age? *Old age*? A time when you have lived so long that you find it impossible to let go.

Ripe, yes it is. Pleasant? No!

Watch the old people on the street. They walk so carefully, so cautious when crossing the road. So worried about their vitamin supplements. So scared of the next minute. Shaking hands, thrown up at the oncoming traffic as they wobble along when what they should wish for is a speeding bus to come along and hit them, hard. Habituated to living in fear of that resilient truth that we speak of. They are running from the wide-open, friendly arms of your resilient truth and its embrace. Running scared. Watching their friends die before them, losing relations, plodding along ever so cautiously...scared that they will break something. Sacred that their time will come. Farting loudly with the highest regard for their own deafness.

Seen some nasty samples, haven't you?

The lust for life is never as severe as it is in old age.

he carried his walking stick for show, it was some excellent wood
Tigers in a forest carved into it...

I must look awesome to the onlooker:
Young kid walking in harmony with old granddad...

We reach the grocers'
Ask for the stuff on our list

*The old lady shopkeeper puts in things in our polyethylene
bags*
Things that we do not want
He clarifies
She carries on
He yells, shouting out for her to stop
And meticulously shouts out the items on our list,
laying it on the counter for her to see
She hears him now
She does not look at the list or at him
She empties the packet per his shouted instructions
'She's hard of hearing!' he says
Not to me, I think
He is speaking to himself
'She cannot hear!' he laughs
I look at him, shaking his head in mirth
*Looking intently at the old woman shopkeeper who does not
look at him, or at the list*
Celebrating her deafness
Celebrating his prowess
while she wobbles around looking for the things that we want.

If you continue to treat it like it were a gift and if you
believe that jumping off the balcony means that you are
throwing it away, you will not see the light.

Won't I?

You will not. Think of a note clearly stating that neither is anybody responsible nor anyone to blame for 'my death'. Will anyone take it seriously?

No. Life is too precious for you to take that note seriously and you start implicating everyone you possibly can for the 'untimely event'! Stop for a moment. Stop to think. What if the guy really meant it? No one to blame. No one responsible! *His* decision. *His* life too precious to waste in anticipation of an obvious, routine, future. That is how much he valued his life. It takes courage. It isn't cowardice. Just because you don't have the courage, and you live to talk about it, and you live to hear about it, you call it cowardice. Because you *can*. It takes courage. It takes belief that this must be the end and that life is not worth living on autopilot.

Such belief cannot stem from unhappiness alone. Want to quit while I'm ahead. What's so damn difficult to grasp? Forget the religious and legal arguments against it. Salvation is simplicity. Salvation is a short story. Salvation is about writing yourself out of the corner. It is about untying the knots, turning things on their head and putting it all in a short, simple sentence.

Or two.

*   *   *

What is the best way to go? You speak about jumping off the balcony. Is that your choice of method?
Haven't thought about the method at all. Jumping off the balcony is messy, isn't it? Unpleasant. It also

disregards the beauty of the human body. You know, *Nau das maans bunan ko laage… chadaria… jhini re jhini…*

That was a lovely one. Nine months…to weave the blanket of our bodies…or the sheet of our bodies…

Yes. To weave the blanket or the sheet on the spinning wheel made of the eight petal lotus…and the five elements as yarn…I loved that bit…
Ashta kamal ka charkha banaya…moorakh mailee kini…

…the fool soiled it…

I wonder…are these the same chakras that they refer to when you meditate?

No. Those are seven chakras or centres of energy, aren't they? And in this hymn, they are referring to a spinning wheel made of the lotus with eight petals or lotuses and there was something about the eight lotuses or latent energies interacting with the seven or eight energy centres of the body. Maybe they are the same. Who knows!
Hmmm. You know for all the deep meaning that there is to what God and man create, I sure have a shallow disposition. My grasp is limited, I now realize, to the literal. I am lazy and don't seem to care for a deep understanding of…anything. Not law. Not politics. Not religion. Not literature…You know what my one take from this hymn was? Do you know which part of my life it affected?

Tell me.

I didn't get a tattoo. Because that would spoil the sheet or blanket that it took nine months to weave...a *tattoo*. And I used the hymn and its literal meaning to scorn at anyone who did get a tattoo in college. I prided in being uncool and all that, although some of my listeners were pretty impressed with my knowledge, you know? I know this hymn by Kabir that they all had heard but did not remember! Boy! Was I the intelligent one! But I don't fool me...I was such a phony. I am such a phony.

Maybe the method one chooses has something to do with the state of one's mind? But, we cannot be sure about these things. I mean, when you hang or throw yourself off, or poison yourself, these must be the forms chosen by the unhappy, depressed. Or possibly I am wrong. Maybe because access to the materials is so bloody limited, they could be used by anyone, I guess.

Between a balcony and a mountain, I would choose the mountain. That is less messy and also a beautiful fall, with a view, and all. Materially different from jumping off the balcony, you know? And the fact that there would be little need to...uh...clean up, and all. There is such an inelegance to jumping off the balcony. Too much drama. And an inconvenient mess. A most unromantic option because all you wanted was the appropriate height. So you chose a balcony or the roof. Too many people around. Too many strangers likely witnessing something that is personal. I think it is also reflective of depression. Yep, a cliff's prettier. But then, who am I to judge?

Also, it gives one enough time to regret the jump!

Perhaps. Maybe even enough time to then reaffirm that the jump was the right thing to do. Who knows?

And cutting your wrists? Setting yourself on fire?

Add cutting your wrists to my list of the unhappy or depressed. I don't think that the depressed should terminate things at all. They should get that help that everyone says they should. They have ripped suicide off its credibility as a decision that sensible, sane people could make, as a matter of *choice*. There is so much more to the idea! Why does it only have to be people who are in a corner in life? Why does it have to be the end to the *suffering*, which suffering, the watching crowd will dismiss as frivolous in any case? You can hear them say, 'Oh! He failed an exam, so what?' or 'Alright, so she got dumped, but was it the end of the world? No!' And they are right, you know? It isn't the end of the world.

Why is it not a beginning? Just like all of dying is? Fire. I like that. Self-immolation. One of the five great elements in Hinduism. But, I think that is something one would do when one has a point to make, which is why it seems to be the favoured method amongst protestors. I will say that blasting oneself off from the kitchen using

a gas leak is pretty cool, too. Must be messy afterwards but it is still cool. Go out with a bang! I don't like hanging. Maybe because that is how they do the death penalty in India. Gives the impression that you're punishing the people close to you or something.
Drowning?

Drowning…no…drowning is different. I like that, you know? Involves a key element of nature. And I am Piscean.

Drowning is like being shot at. Or no, it was being shot at that was like diving into a pool of cold water or something. You know, *Illusions*? I wonder what happened to Richard Bach. Don't hear of him these days. What a splash he had made with those books of his. The blue feather on a black background on the cover, do you remember it? The blue feather. A sign.

You cannot let go.

Once you are done with your life's work, once you have had enough and want to move on… to the next life. Once you have finished your best symphony, composed the best song you that you ever will, written the most honest prose that you ever will…

How do you know that you will not be inspired by a new beat? How do you know that you will not write about a sight that you see ten years from now? How do you know that the life you thought was a lemon will not ripen into a sweet orange?

I don't like sweet oranges. I prefer the sour ones. The ones that gave rise to etymological concerns because they are not orange on the outside but green with taut skin. Taut fibers, which I puncture with my thumb. When I rip the peel off, there are no flocculent parts that start to drip. The crisp slicing and crunch of a healthy, just-before-it turned-sweet orange interspersed with the raw bitterness of its fibers.

How do you know that you will not change to preferring sweet to the sour that you love so much today? How will you turn around to stare down the wrong path that you took and kick yourself? How will you share the story of your joys and your misery with your children? You cannot let go and you are bad at goodbyes.

Yes. I know. I am.

You still wake up to dreaming about Coco. You have not forgotten her.

I miss her. But I don't want her back. I know that she is gone. I resigned myself to her death many years ago. When I started seeing what the signs were really telling me.

she used to disappear sometimes when the noisy fire crackers frightened her
she did not come back…this time
we searched the city

put her picture in the papers
she was famous

I saw her everywhere…in a flash with her peer scrounging
garbage dumps
disappearing   around   street   corners…a   flash   of
tail…everywhere

I think I was mad because I would see a small heap in
the middle of the road and fret that it was her…but it
wasn't her, ever…it was either another animal… mostly
cats, nine lives up, or just discarded clothes. I don't
know how these clothes reach the middle of the road.
Do people strip while travelling? Or do they just dump
them, right there in a heap? It is quite disconcerting. You
start wondering who wore those clothes and all.
When did you know?

I *had* started to see the signs but I had refused to
acknowledge them. Her rainbow collar that we had got
her for her first birthday, you remember it? It looked
perfect against her shiny black…it started to wear
away…too quickly. It had been hanging on a hook in
Coco's corner and one day, the nylon threads that had
held on so firmly seemed to give way. Just like that.

my hands are shaking
I am stitching them up…the frayed threads
darning…they had tried to teach me in school…
nothing that can't be mended
the steel buckle gleams as if it were new
and at that moment, hope shines with it…

she will be back, as always, she was just scared of the firecrackers, like always, I think.

With signs, you have to be able to discern what it is that you *want* to see and what it is that the universe is actually showing you. Is it the frayed collar that you should be focusing on, or the shining steel buckle that you are seeing?

Hint: if you spot the shining steel buckle after the frayed threads gave you a scare, you are cheating. But it is alright to cling to hope for as long as you need to. You will give up eventually when hope gives up on you.

One day only the buckle hung from the hook. The collar was gone. It was lying on the floor. That moment I stopped praying for her to come back. I had my peace. I had wondered around then if there was a heaven and if she was there. I looked at the sky and saw wisps of clean white cloud taking the shape of Coco, running…her half-cocked ears, resisting the wind, like disproportionately small wings that were helping her fly…her happy tail, all spruced up and waving at me…I saw her in the sky…the black dog of uncertain descent but definitely part-Alsatian had morphed into a wispy white angel. I had my peace.

Closure.

Closure. It is important, isn't it? The whole thing about letting go…stuff left undone, things unsaid, I suppose. I suppose one must leave a note. Say goodbye. I wouldn't want them to keep wondering 'why'…yes, must leave a note. It *is* the sky that I connect with, isn't it? The stars and clouds…I think it is because we are conditioned to think of heaven up there. We keep looking up.

The sky in Bombay shows no signs at all! And that, when you can see it past the sky scrapers.

Yes. You cannot really look up at the sky and walk around here even if it were an accessible sky.

The crowd would shove you relentlessly and you'd probably collide with a pole, pedestrian or hawker.

Or get honked out of your delirium by an impatient bus…

CHAPTER 5
A Place Called Delirium

You know, in Brussels there was this young guy. Indian. With the please-fit-me-in accent that they all get themselves. He told me about a place I should visit at the Grand Place. A place called Delirium. "They serve a thousand types of beer…"

"Wow!"

What else could I say? It was a formal first meeting and we were trying to make a connection so that we could write a warm note or two as post-scripts to the post-meeting follow up correspondence. Networking. I let him believe that a thousand types of beer was impressive. That I would drink them all. That I actually *liked* beer.

I had to go there, you know. Imagine…a place called Delirium.

It's like calling a place 'Twilight', you know? I like this abstract mating of nothing and everything, could-be-this-could-be-that sort of name for people, and things.

The possibilities in contradiction and vagueness!

I walked and walked and I swear that my heart was beating hard. It was going to be a revelation. A place called 'Delirium'.

And there was the beer…

What? No. The thousand types of beer don't mean anything. I wasn't looking for beer, okay?

Anyway, I asked this girl smoking outside a bar for a place called 'Delirium' and she pointed it out to me. 'Fourth place on the left'. So, it existed. It was real! And I was close. Fourth place on the left.

It was just another a restaurant. Straight walls, just a bar with bar stools…no barrels storing mysterious and exotic concoctions, no dark corners that became black holes because of very bright lighting…I stepped into what should have been the *sanctum sanctorum*.
Just a beer shop, man! Just that. Routine wood-effect bar and bottles to back it. Dispensers.

'What's so bloody delirious about this place?' I shouted in my head at the bartender who shot-smiled me a welcome 'I'm out.'

I didn't stay long enough to remember more. Cafés Mondegar and Leopold on Colaba Causeway are more delirious than Delirium in the Grand Place. And I don't think they serve more than three types of beer.

What did I expect? I don't know.

An opium den. A secret island. Something illegal that a select few accessed. Who wants a beer bar, shop selling beer? Disappointing.

Why?

Don't ask me why! Go find the place for yourself and see.

Was the bloody Gujarati excitedly exaggerating about the thousand types of beer?
I Googled it. He wasn't. Anyway, legend has it that the place is named after a beer called Delirium Tremens. You know, withdrawal symptoms from alcohol abuse and associated hallucinations or something?

Whatever.

I know that it's supposed to be witty to name an alcohol like that, and I would have laughed at it in a parallel life, in another world, where I also enjoyed beer. But it just didn't work for me that day. You know what killed me, though? When I stepped out into the disappointed street, I took a last look at the façade, at the name of the place – a blue screen background and a pink elephant on it and of course, pinky letters that spelt 'Delirium'. A *pink* elephant! *Pink*…

Was the elephant tottering?

No. He was just…pink. Could've been dancing a slow dance but he wasn't *tottering*. They had made him cute. In my other world, where I like beer, I would love that this represented hallucinations symptomatic of Delirium Tremens.

In this world, I want to know how different people could imagine the same pinky elephant when they were experiencing delirium tremens? Not logical. I died.

Was it a she-elephant? A cow.

I don't know. Is that even relevant?

*   *   *

Shall we go for a walk? It is 7 P.M. already. We have two hours and fifteen minutes before Debbie gets here to usurp my peace and it is starting to get dark. I know what, I'll make her cook!

Just like old times.

Just like old times.

Where are we headed? I don't know. Not the BPT Garden at this time…it gets depressing so late in the evening. Let's just walk. To nowhere, you know? There is no clear air around here so don't expect it to clear your head, or your system, but let's walk so that we can share a drink called loneliness *but it's better than drinking alone!*

Tra la la la…God! I love the song. *Piano Man.*
Which reminds me. What about the gin and tonic? Did we forget about it? *Do* we forget about it? It isn't such a big deal as we're making it out to be, is it? Just one drink. It can do no harm. Is it too early for a quick one?

No. This is one drink that may be had at any time of the day.

I never put the tonic in the fridge.

Once we are back, then?

Yes, but we must return before Debbie.

Why? She got it for you, didn't she? She knows.

You are right. How did that slip my mind? She knows. She might continue to be a pain in the ass about it but she does know. I don't have to be alone…

You aren't alone, sweetheart. We don't have to be alone.
I'm going to grab an apple and some bread before we step out. Haven't eaten forever. I have a question. When

we step out, like now, in the elevator, what will people see? Two women walking into the elevator and out of the gate? Or is it just I who can see you? What will Debbie see, when she is here, with us?

It will be like it always has been. There will be two of us.

Hmm. So, that means only I see you, and that I alone hear you. Do people see me speaking to you?

Sometimes, I suppose, when they care to notice.

They must think me mad.

Yes.

I am not mad!

No. Besides, a lot of our talking is in the head.

*   *   *

Good thing the elevator attendant isn't in. Picture me on a train, crowded with strangers. I strum lightly on my guitar. They gather around me. In Kenny Rogers' voice, I sing,

On a warm summer's eve
On a train bound for nowhere
I met up with the gambler
We were both too tired to sleep…

You got to know when to hold 'em, know when to fold 'em,

Know when to walk away, know when to run
You never count your money when you're sittin' at the table
There'll be time enough for countin' when the dealin's done...

Hmmm hmmm hmmm hmmm hmm hmmm...
And the best that you can hope for is to die in your sleep.

You know, that's it, isn't it. What is the best that you can hope for?

World peace?

No.

The end to global warming?

No.

An end to hatred and intolerance?

No.
An end?

And that you don't see it coming.

Die in your sleep.

'Cause every hand's a winner and every hand's a loser
And the best that you can hope for is to die in your sleep...

It freaks me out, you know? What the world's coming to. Global warming, climate change, terrorism, the economic downturn... And I keep thinking that there will be our children and our children's children like that child's voice speaks at the beginning of *Heal the World*...and what is their future going to be? What has man made of man?

To her fair works did Nature link
The human soul that through me ran;
And much it grieved my heart to think
What man has made of man.

Great works, wasn't it? Not *fair* works?

Great...fair...same difference.
Be careful where you step. All the human feces on the sidewalks of Colaba. Neither great nor fair, and Nature has still linked us to this, too now, hasn't she?

*   *   *

the results will be out tomorrow
which means that when he was speaking to Mum, he must've been discussing my performance in math...
they were talking with too much intensity for it to be an exchange of civilities
The education system
does not allow for diversity, individuality...
I cannot do math

When I see the poor, I feel compassion

More compassion than the other students are even capable of imagining
I am wasting my time studying
And I am going to open up about the way that I feel with Mum

It is time that she knew that I am suffocating
Math isn't even the point
All my education cannot prepare me for the battles that I am going to fight
For the war that I am going to declare on all human suffering…

And my tears, will be proof of how strongly I feel
I know that she will freak out

But my conviction will give her strength
I can hear her footsteps. She is walking towards my room
she is going to be so worried when she sees me like this
Thinking about the poor and the hungry…the naked and the dead
And weeping alone into my pillow

'You are the only girl to have failed Math,' Mum declares…
That had made no sense. It was a weird batch that year.
Imagine girls excelling in Math. Imagine my failing it.

Anyway, it was just a half yearly. I was a fraud, as usual.

Liar.

I was meant for great things. I was going to change the world, to lead. The songs that we listened to, created a storm inside me, I was a live volcano that forgot to erupt. What I wouldn't do to *Heal the World* with Michael Jackson! I did nothing.

When I look back at my life, many years from now, it will be a series of things that did not happen. I can see clearly now. No great achievement, a mediocre life, spent amidst mediocrity, with no attempts made to rise up or stand out. No great friendships to boast about, no anecdotes to tell, no fascinating foes. Just one long string of everyday occurrences, each as uneventful as the next. Nothing lost, nothing found. No great victories, no downright failure.

Not even in Math.

Not even in Math. It was a half-yearly examination that I had failed. The finals carried me through with a 55 per cent. 55. The ordinariness of such a number. Can it have been more ordinary? Neither here nor there.

I am not phenomenally beautiful, I am not ugly. I am a good lawyer. I will not be a great lawyer. I have intelligence, no genius. And I cannot, objectively speaking, be called an idiot. My life has seen no great sorrows, no tragedy that could move me, galvanize my doing…more…so much more. Equally, I have known no profound happiness beyond the ordinary. A few moments here and there that would satisfy a moron have worked for me. Only a fool can lie to himself convincingly enough. I am no fool. I do know that I am a liar. I can catch these lies. They don't fool me. Not for a minute.

So, were you to die today, you would be terribly dissatisfied, wouldn't you? Unhappy, maybe?

No! No! No! You don't fool me with that. I would die because I was *bored*, at best. Merely because I realize that I have lived an ordinary life does not make me unhappy. I could count my blessings just as much as the next person and we would be very pleased with the score. No. I would jump from a cliff today, now, because I am certain of the future, and how it will turn out and most importantly, I am certain that in other worlds, in parallel lives, I am doing all the extraordinary things that zoom across my mind every day. I can see those things happening and they are so real, they must be happening. I can feel, I know, I hear the applause, the appreciation and the passion of the lives that I have not lived in this lifetime. I would not be sad to give this one up because I know that all of those possibilities are in fact real. Reality. Realities?

Reality. Whatever.

My dreams, my imagination, my thoughts are one with the universe, without my always knowing it, I am aware of my link to Her great, or fair works. And this makes me happy. I am tired of the tediousness that I have chosen. This is where it should stop. Now. Today.

Possibly, tomorrow. Once I have had the time to figure the logistics out. There are no new routes to be discovered, no continents left unexplored, depleting rain forests, no peaks left unconquered and no story left untold. I would chase new species of sea creatures, insects...or a new variety of plant life, if I cared any less than I do now for that sort of thing.

I know that I have nothing to show for it in this life and this world but then...listen carefully, nobody's asking for it.

CHAPTER 6
NIGHT

I wonder what's behind all of these buildings with all of these shops. Houses and houses and homes and tenants. Such a crowd. More new buildings, more people. More shit on the pavements. The scent of hardware stores, timber markets, sweets and wafers and savories all inextricably tied up. The picture framers…all of them together. They don't use wood around here anymore. Just fiber. Very practical. Very synthetic. Very dead Like the façade of all of these buildings, holding together homes, that look symmetrical and organized and firm but they are like a sheet of cheap, synthetic chinon fabric, which can rip any time and which shines with artifice trying so hard to be the genuine chiffon that it is not…it never fooled me. I know wood from fiber. I know the look and feel of chiffon…

Look in through those windows dressed with the cheapest available fabric. See the cluttered living of those souls in space that is so constrained it could snuff the life out of you. The women who stare out of those windows into these filthy streets, they are dead. Look at their eyes. Not brooding, not thinking, staring blankly back at my stare. No connection. The noise from the street is their idea of escape from the cacophony of their crowded houses. This is their bondage. Bursting at the seams. A single bomb would finish many hundreds. A wave, some thousands.

*   *   *

I have one more reason to end it. And that is this – I do not have the courage.

I cannot see them leave me here alone. I cannot wait for the inevitable.

Karan was dazed that morning. He was irritable.
We're in the college canteen
We look at each other
I grin
I like him like this...rude, obnoxious, offensive
I like him like this because I will not marry him;
I will not suffer this mood...his bullshit...

I have the sense to keep my bloody distance.
I am not nosey.
I wish everyone stopped asking him what the matter was
God! He's not alright, can't you see?
If he hasn't come looking for you to tell you his sorrows, then he probably will not confide in you when you ask, now will he?

And it is these very people, who would make way for him,
avoid him, and stand at a distance from him, if Karan were
wailing loudly…telling them about his great sorrow.
They would think him mad and run a mile away from him.
These same people. Flies.
They hover around us, concerned for him.
They ask me what's wrong with him…
I shrug. How should I know?
I am not a fly.

We are alone at the table now because the Lion has snarled
away all the Hyenas
He is smoking…
his hands are not steady,
he glances at me to see if I have noticed,
'I had a fucked up dream this morning. I saw my mother
dead.'

'Just a dream, Karan.'
'Of course it was! I called home when I woke up. But that
image was so bloody real. That is how it will be, I know, and I
cannot stop thinking about it. She is lying there and I am
looking at her. The image has not left me. I thought one does
not remember dreams. Was this a dream? Or was it something
that I was seeing, have I willed it to happen or something?'

'I remember my dreams all the time. Of course you haven't
willed it but it is, it is… inevitable, no? Did you have the
dream in the morning? I mean, when you snapped out of
it…was it morning?'

'Why?' he asks more screwed up than he was a minute ago
'No reason. Not important.'

'They come true, no? That's what they say, don't they?
Morning dreams come true…'
I say, 'Don't screw your mind.'
But I already did that for him, didn't I?

*   *   *

Memory has a habit of leaping out at you from hidden corners. It appears, when you least expect it, in spurts and extracts.

I know. What surprises you most is how you remember what happened, how you cannot remember all of it and what portion of the past you do end up remembering. It could be the minutest detail, so irrelevant in that past that becomes important in this present – the way he had looked, the way he looked at you, the din of voices, a snippet of what was said, how lovely it smelt, how cold it felt.

They flash upon the inward eye…that's what he meant. Longfellow. Wordsworth? It is not always the bliss of bloody solitude. It's hell most of the time.

To be able to forget is one of the greatest freedoms of the human mind. What would you do if you were not able to say, 'I forgot to do my homework?'

Which is why I continued to forget my homework even when it was unpardonable because I forgot the painful humiliation of it all.

Maybe you realized, when you remembered, that it wasn't as bad as it had seemed. Your memory changed the way it had felt.

Memory has a life of its own. I remember Baba dancing for us but the memory makes me sad now. I was happy when it was...forming? Is this how he looked? As I see him now.

Round and round, 'I'm-a-tea-pot pose', his hand on top of his head, the other hand holding his waist, swaying clumsily...

Why did we laugh so much?

I forgot to remember to forget...Presley?

Nah. Beatles.

To forget, is charming, socially, when you are telling a story and want to get to the point – forget the details, twist events a little, exaggerate, drawing equally upon memory and imagination.

Imagine that your entire life, all your experiences, all the faces that you know, all the faces that you don't know, everything about you, all your thoughts, perceptions, beliefs and understanding – the sum of your existence, is the ocean. It is the source of memory.
Waves are memory. No two waves are the same.

The ocean responds to an external force. It rises and falls. The tides are dreams.

And on the ocean, is a surfer, waiting for spilling breakers and plunging breakers, so that he can glide into the air tube as the crest of the wave folds over. A good tide and excellent wind will make his day. The surfer is imagination.

I like that. He could emerge from the air pocket gracefully riding the wave as it dies amidst the skipping foam on the shore, or he could fall, tripping on the power of the sea, crashing onto the waiting shore with a mad rush of foam.

Daydreams are imagination. We see them under controlled conditions with our eyes open and our senses, awake. Night time dreams let imagination go wild. The sub-conscious takes over, drawing from the vast ocean of memory and more – the tides affected by the external force.

And some try and interpret them but much depends upon the memory of the dreamer, doesn't it? A conscious recollection of what the sub-conscious imagined is after all what he will tell the interpreter.

Do your dreams add up? Is there a message in them for you?

If you are connected to the universe, linked to the great…fair or whatever works, then…don't you think that is true? Interesting. I could ask an interpreter but I will not, I do not have the time and lack curiosity. Maybe, even faith.

*   *   *

I love the junk, trinkets and souvenirs available on Colaba Causeway.

When I first came to Bombay, I used to make a mental list of the things that I would buy from here and where I would put them in my imaginary house.

I would visit people's houses and dress them up with all the things that I had picked up from here in my mind.

And now, now that I have that house, I don't care to crowd it with trinkets because of the dust that the clutter would no doubt gather. Then, there are the lizards that would love the mess and lay their eggs in it.
Is that me?

Yes. My phone. Debbie calling.

"Hullo? I can't hear you, Deb…too much noise!

So why should that delay you?

Nine? Not before that?

No. Whatever. What do you want to do for dinner? Will you cook for us?

Alright. You know, I am out myself and I should really be eating on time and all. So we'll take it as it comes.

No. I am not near you. I am at Colaba.

Walking. Need to walk. Clear my head. I'll see you. Just call me when you're leaving. Maybe you can pick me up from wherever I am.

Yep. Bye!"

Shall I skip the plan about Debbie cooking and order takeaway from Leopold's? *Chicken biryani*, maybe? Buzzing as usual.

I don't like Leopold's anymore. It has changed. The night club especially, I mean. This is where I saw those blacks dancing with their own reflections in the mirrors. And the way that they move, just…it is supposed to be awesome and I am supposed to go on and on about how awesome it is to be able to move like that but I don't…

Am I a prude? Am I lying to myself? Can I see myself doing it?

Who knows, right?

Yes. That's right. I am a fake. I know. I am a *Hibiscus*. Not an *Allamanda*.

I can't take night clubs anymore. How are shoving, and being shoved and touching bodies, getting to the bar and pleading for the barman's attention, and dancing without space to move, cool?

That is it! Ha! Modern dancing has evolved because there is no room to waltz and whirl and swirl and trot, where people congregate these days. That is why their savage dancing is in. A result of urbanization and sheer bloody lack of space. You may know how to jive but I challenge you to try that at one of these discs. We seem to be heading towards the Gateway of India. Isn't that fantastic?

It is supposed to be, isn't it? Would one feel the same way when walking towards other landmarks in the world? The Washington Monument? Big Ben? The Eiffel Tower?

And yet. I couldn't give a damn.

The crowd.

That's it. The crowd, the sheer bloody crowd kills it for me. A monument is something that you see from afar. You should have time, and space, to think about it. Possibly, admire it.

Constant cacophony makes it impossible to *think*. I could never read the inscription on it and on the plaque or whatever near it. No. Too many people shoving past me, hurrying for the ferry ride, selling stuff, asking me if I wanted an instant photo, speaking…talking in too many languages that I don't like the sound of.

Look at the water lapping at the side of the embankments. Complaining on and on about the reclamation…beating its head against the wall. I understand this…no space to make a decent wave…no space to think. So it pushes against the walls of the embankment and the walls nudge it back. Sometimes, there is a spray for walkers to enjoy…the futile battle with the wall. Many people look over. Sometimes, they fall over and have to be rescued. Some have drowned. There are quite a few swimmers around, at all times, if one goes by the news reports. And these swimmers are perpetually foiling whatever plans the person looking over the embankment may have had. They are the enemy.

Would you dive into that water to save someone?

I guess. Why not? I suppose, if no one else did within a minute of said someone toppling over, sure. But it is rather murky and gray. One sees the litter and crap floating on it. I don't know. I mean, I guess, to save a life one
would do it but, you know…it is quite filthy.

Not the place that you would choose to drown in, then?

That is a thought. Would I? I cannot say. I mean, not everyone has the luxury of a river or stream running conveniently close by to actually organize the grand sinking. We cannot all boast of Ms. Woolf's fortune, can we now? But this is a thought...

late evening, the crowd is thinning,
cops don't pay that much attention
to people standing awfully close to the walls or leaning over...
I jump in.
Dark-skinned young boys appear from nowhere, dive in and
swim towards me

A shout goes around...someone fell in... someone leaped in?
Someone is drowning! Someone's being rescued!

The dispersing crowd rushes back.
They have to see this! What an interesting story! What luck!

The divers have gotten to me by now.
No use resisting them...

And the current state of the law would prevent anyone in a right state of mind from owning up to having attempted *suicide*. The cops would be sympathetic. They realize that people need help not harassment, especially when said people are not gays holding hands in a sparsely populated park.

I would say that I fell in as I bent over, or that I was too distracted sitting on the wall and leaned over because I thought that I saw a mermaid.

And, I would be news…with the brave divers, their pictures splattered across the Mumbai's dailies. They wouldn't put my photo in but they'd call my husband. And, I suppose, the people in the office would know.

And if nobody dived in, you would probably swim out of it, with a few stringy polyethylene bags and rags clinging to your limbs.

Hurdles indeed. I may just stuff my jacket with stones to ensure the sinking.
You will unzip the jacket and let it sink while you swim away, and out. The body fights the mind. It cannot be that there is no moment, however short, when you fight your decision. Possibly, regret it. You will fight yourself to survive, if you have to.
Then, like Houdini, let me devise a mechanism to lock in the stones and ensure that they weigh me down. Like a bag or something that I could carry on my back. Lock it, chain it to myself and throw in the key before jumping in. There. Does that satisfy you?

Good idea. You know, what I can immediately think of is the cobblestones that they are using all over the city.

Yes! I tried to pick one up to put a flowerpot on when those crows were making it impossible for me to see my ixoras…it was bloody heavy.

We'd have to take a cab…can't carry those stones all the way walking…no way in hell…will need at least two of them to make them count…buoyancy and all that. Cab it. Haul the heavy backpack across to the edge, chain it to self, will seem like I am fidgeting with my baggage, to the general onlooker. Then, be quick. Real fast.

What about the baby? Do I have the right to make that decision? The *ratio* in *Roe vs Wade* is not in my favour, is it? It isn't my decision. We did not think of this, did we? Carry those cobblestones in a backpack? How can it be done in this...*state*? How do I even get on to the embankment's wall? Hullo! How did we miss this? Such detailed planning and I am constrained. Terribly constrained. I don't understand how women gloat over their unborn kids...

Aside from a physical hindrance to some of my existence, I feel nothing. When it moves, I want to tap my tummy and communicate with it, but it does not know me. And I don't know it. Can you love a fetus? I need to read *Roe vs Wade* again. How out of touch I am with Women's Studies...And I was so proud of that paper that I had published, 'Motherhood: the Defined and Constraining Norm'. So true. So true. Nobody had understood it. But it was published in a leading journal, wasn't it? Anyway, I know what I wrote. And no, I don't need to read *Roe vs Wade* again. The personal is not political.

That is right. I will carry out my plans...sooner or later. Won't I conform to the defined norm? Just this little decision...is it before or after? Or will a baby constrain my thinking...will I chicken out of it once I hold a child in my arms? Will I succumb to the lure of this material world? And remain chained to the mediocrity of my existence?

I will be a mediocre mother. The word that has come to define me. Mediocre. And how I hate it. I would much rather not exist. Drowning. It's like being shot at, no? Or was it being shot at that's like jumping into cold water? It is like returning to the womb…the watery grave…a long dunking…there will be some moments…some minutes when you will fight…but then, water will find its course…they say that the oxygen runs out pretty soon and you are actually unconscious at the time that you 'drown'. It is all quite painless and all, which makes sense because, in a way, it's a return to the element that holds you for nine months and all that jazz.

The note will just say, 'I'm happy. See you in our other lives.' There should be a note. Closure. Maybe it could say, 'I'm not unhappy. I am alright…' and the rest. Maybe a piece requesting the cops not to bother anyone and stuff.

I just hope that they pull me out before I bloat. That would make water absolutely perfect. I have to pee. All this thought of water and I really have to go.

Oh! My God. It will be nine thirty soon. Debbie will reach home before me. Why the hell hasn't she called?

Better grab a cab and head home to welcome her. Maybe call her to Leopold's and get the *Biryani*. Cannot wait an hour for her to cook…I am supposed to be eating at the right time. Can't be so bloody spaced out about this stuff. Debbie did not jump at the idea of her cooking when I mentioned it, anyway. Old times or not.

The question is this: shall I hold it or shall I go? I get nervous about this stuff after reading that darned book. It said, *'you got to go when you got to go'*. Or something like that. Being pregnant and trying to be nonchalant about it is bloody impossible. I am scared. I cannot hold my breath too long when I swim because I am so scared of what might happen. And I just can't hold it anymore. Thankfully, there is the Taj, and the nice smelling toilets and the hand lotion after one is done washing up.

And the smiling attendants.
They should really not be there. I mean, you need space and privacy in the loo and when you know that they are there, you make a single sound and they can guess what's happening behind that door. And I am not, in a position, in my current state, to lean forward to ensure against the loud shushing, the whispered tinkling on the ceramic and that merry bubbly babbling of fluid against fluid…

Curse the drowning. Isn't it easier to jump in front of a moving train? Or to get hit by a bus?

*   *   *

I never understood the allure of this building.

Again, not cool. Everyone speaks so fondly of the Taj. I think that it is just overhyped and a way for people to reconcile the cash that they blow up here with the real value that it brings you. I can never speak fondly of it and have to work very hard on bringing my eyes to gleam with the fake fondness of the average Mumbaikar when speaking about this allegedly iconic hotel. Just another old building that got taken better care of than the others, that's all. Opulent. What did you expect?

India, of the cheap labour and staff that will smile. India – of the wanting sense of humor, and of the lacking intellect, and the fake sweetness to make up for it all.

The usual question when you see them out to the elevator… where are you staying?
The Taj. They are never embarrassed to answer.
When they aren't staying there, they mumble something about being close to the airport…it could be any of all those other hotels…why do they assume that I care?
The Taj! I beam back at them.
Lovely hotel.
Where can we shop? We'll have a few hours tomorrow.
Colaba Causeway… trinkets…the Lonely Planet…Fab India…the usual crap.
Make a connection. Make a connection and hope that it will pay off with a, fantastic mother-of-all referrals…catapulting you to partnership…

*   *   *

So what if I haven't had more than a coffee at the Coffee Shop, ever? And it wasn't so great, either. It is just another hotel. Another con job where things are more expensive than they ought to be and therefore, everyone smiles at you.

Ashish has a coaster from the Harbour Bar

He framed it for his desk

I like it.

The coaster's got this world-mappy-oceany sort of thing printed on it and all...

I collect coasters. From everywhere. Maybe they'll give me a couple if I ask them. On my way out. It's right opposite the toilets. And here I go. Service with a smile.

She is smiling at me. Even sweeter than usual. Because of the way that I look. She must be a mom herself. The other guests are just snoots. I can look like that, too. When I have a bucket of makeup on. Assholes.

I haven't thought of names. We haven't discussed them.

A mother has the undisputed, superior right to name the child. And the only person who can challenge that decision is the child himself. Nobody else. Suggestions are welcome but will be used only if acceptable to the mother. The woman's right is absolute.

Not in half the cultures of the world.

But, it is absolute. It should be. And I don't rely upon judgments of the United States Supreme Court to tell you that…except when it suits me…and, for Moot Courts and debating competitions.

Do you want a father stuck with calling you a name that he never liked?

I think that is how it will be with 'Atharva'. Which is why I haven't discussed it with him.

I have been Googling and Googling for names but just cannot find one. None of them are…none of them are…What a queue. All the doors are locked. Come on! Come on! I have to go!

It is a waste bringing children into the world. I see how protective parents are about their kids and all. Don't their hearts stop when they see the amount of garbage on the streets? And climate change? Why are we still procreating? With what right? What do we think is going to come of it all? The world as we know it will be worse in the coming years, there will be destruction and earthquakes and tidal waves and all that. And we will have the satisfaction of knowing that we sent into the world, this horrid world, our blood, our progeny. We don't care enough for our children.

We should all lay back and die.

And before we do that, we should ensure that we haven't done anything to prolong the agony. No issues. No spouses. No partners. Sterile existence structured to let go. We have done enough harm, enough damage.

Now, let the other lives take over. This one, on this planet, is finished.

God! What are these women doing? Not a single tell-tale sound! No welcome squirting of the toilet-hand-spray no shuffling of garments. Wait. There are no hand- in here. Right. Another thing I hate about Indian hotels. What are you trying to prove? That you don't wash and that you only wipe? So embarrassed to be Eastern. Try that in your homes, jerks. Just try it. I want to see the look on your parents' faces when you design a home with no hand-sprays in the toilets. Phonies.

No sound. No sound. No rumbling of the toilet paper handle! Just the sound of my voice in my head. And all the other voices in my head. When will they come out? Shall I knock? I should sit. My legs hurt.

Its 9:30 P.M.! For Christ's sake! Damn it. Is my watch fast? I had set it to faster, but I don't remember whether it was by ten or fifteen minutes...I can never remember...which is good because if I did, I wouldn't be able to cheat myself into believing I'm late...Finally. Someone flushed. Rustling of garments. Too slow. Too slow. Hurry up, woman.

I cannot hold on any more.

Click. Door knob.

There she is. Fat ass. I hope she hasn't left it stinking inside. I cannot wait a second to allow the stench time to disperse!

Made it!

Unbuckle.

Strip.

Whoosh.

Don't care if it is as loud as a trumpet. Just don't bloody care.

Such a rush. Orgasmic. Whew! Much better. Now, I must rush home.

I have been thinking. How do you imagine your kid? I mean, if it's a boy, will he be like Mr. Darcy? A very proper, decent sort of young man? And, if it's a girl, would she be like Eliza Bennet? Sharp tongued. Witty. Prejudiced?

I have never thought of it like that. Haven't had the time, have I? I haven't thought of it at all, actually. It has just been one transaction after another and a good lot of opinion work. When you are thinking about the things that trigger the Takeover Code, you don't fantasize about unborn kids.

You have today…

Today is almost done, isn't it? The sun has set. Debbie will be home. I don't know why she hasn't called me yet.

And this is it. He will be back tomorrow and I will be back in the office fulfilling my promises made today to the Mentoring-Fishing-Partner. Or not. No. I will try. I have to.

Then, there is the issue of the cobblestones and the backpack…

Yes. There is that, too. This is becoming a logistical nightmare. How does the method matter? I think that a moving train would work just fine, now.

We should take one of the street exits. Past the staircase, I think. The Lobby is in the opposite direction to Destination Home, plus it's so crowded. I could walk out of one of these other exits and catch a cab. Will call Debbie from the cab.

Wasn't there an exit straight out of the Harbour Bar?

I don't remember. In any case, I am so not walking into and out of the Bar's street exit! Don't be an ass. We'll look like fools. Just go right. Towards the Mont Blanc store that you will never buy from.

Hey! We forgot the coasters! The Harbour Bar coasters…!

Right! Let me go back. They are usually so bloody obliging at these hotels…need that coaster…
RAT-A-TAT-TAT-TAT-TAT-TAT…

What is that sound? How strange. It seems so close. And real. And still…

DHAG-DHAG-DHAG-DHAG-…

It is from a dream…far away…

My dream…

The one that keeps repeating itself. I am imagining things. I am going mad. First I dream up an imaginary friend. Now, this sound. It's getting out of control…and my hands are cold…and sweating…and my heart is beating fast…

constant, scary, deafening gunfire…

Footsteps. Someone is chasing me.

Be alert. Be alert. Be alert!
Why chase me?

DHAG-DHAG-DHAG-DHAG-…

What's happening…?

Someone is chasing me…

Don't go into the Bar. Turn around. Turn away. Run.

But I can't. My legs are heavy. I want to sit down.

TAT-TAT-TAT-TAT-TAT- …

Why would he chase me? That man? He's freaking me out? What does he want…?

He's been shot? Been shot?

Been shot. Been shot. Been shot.

I cannot move. My legs are heavy. I am heavy. I am carrying this weight…I am frozen…

Constant. Constant. Gunfire.
RATATATTATTATTATTAT…DHGDHGDHGDHGDH GDHGDHGDHG…

Please move…move…move…move…move…move…

I cannot…

They are screaming…

I know…But I cannot hear them…why are they shooting me?
I am the target…

Have to find my way out…have to. Have to. Have to.

I can think…I am thinking…I haven't lost it…I am not mad…I can think…I am thinking…

Find a nook…find a cranny…find a vertex. An angle. A shelter. Take a moment. RUN. Run away.

They're firing at me…? These are gunshots…this is not a movie…this is not a dream.

*   *   *

The gallery of photos of American Presidents and grandly dressed people…black and white. Grey. Each time I walk past it, I wonder if they will put me up there one day. They won't.

I like black and white photography. Why the glass enclosure? Like an aquarium, it looks. All those people staring at you. Fish. In an aquarium. The shops. Fancy pens. Sexy bags. Luxury stores. Dive in.

No. Don't. There is too much glass here. It will stop no one.

>*if I move, they will get me.*
>*if I don't move the bullets will wear down the wood to finish me…*

This is from my dream.

>*DHAG-DHAG-DHAG-DHAG-DHAG!*

Why should I run? Stay here. Being shot at is like diving into cold water. Or something. *Richard Bach. Illusions.* Blue feather. No. Wasn't it in *Jonathan Livingston Seagull?*

No. it was in *Illusions*. The reluctant messiah. He is being told not to laugh on his way to the hanging or something...he is being told what I already know...that this is not the end...it can only be a beginning...what a caterpillar calls the end of the world...a wise man calls a butterfly...it is the beginning...

Shattered glass. There go the aquarium-gallery-of-photos-of-American-Presidents-and-Indian-beauty-queens-in-black-and-white. Shattered glass. The fish fall out, gasping for oxygen. Swallowing poison. But there are no fish. Just black and white photographs of American Presidents and Indian beauty queens.

Broken glass. I walk on the *Boulevard of Broken Dreams*. *I walk alone. I walk alone*. I am tired. I know who sang it...Green Day sang it. Their only song that I know.

Someone will save me. This will end soon. I will wake up. I am so tired. I should sit down. Will it be Frank Hardy? Superman? Mr. Darcy...do I need saving?

Knightley! Knightly! Yes, Mr. Knightley! He should rescue me. He will. Not Darcy.

Oh my God! He is the better person. Not Mr. Darcy! That's right. Not Darcy. It always was Mr. Knightley. Unassuming. Gentle. Honorable. Honest. Considerate. And yes, a single man of large fortune. Large enough, at least. And therefore, it must be *Emma* that I like best...not *Pride & Prejudice*!

This is a discovery.

I have to get out of here. I have to get out of here. This mess.

These glass door shops will not save me. Fish in an aquarium. I have to move. Swim out of the *Boulevard of Broken Dreams*. Have to run. *Forrest*! *Run*! I can hear Jenny shouting it in my head. Run, Forrest. Run!

If I move, they will find me...
    DHAG-DHAG-DHAG-DHAG-DHAG!
    louder than ever, in my face, in my head. NO! NO!
    I must pray. must pray. Oh GOD! please help me!
pray! pray! pray! help me!
I am so sorry...so sorry...

I am not frozen anymore. I am shaking.
Maybe it is a girl? I have been searching for the wrong names, haven't I? That is why I cannot find one that I want to speak to him about.

I have to get out and speak with him. I have to tell him that we must find a pretty name for a girl...
    I can fly.
    when I really need to,
    I can lift off the ground in a twirl. Takes concentration,
a little more-than-the-usual focus...I am flying, hovering over
all of this...I see them, I see me

Even though I am so close to this amazing ceiling of this amazing Hotel… They see me. They shoot me. I have nowhere to go. It does not help that I can fly…

Go back to the ground. Keep trying to escape. Become small. Invisible. No one can see me…

It is time for the magic. Now.

it is happening… the magic.
I am becoming small. invisible
smaller and smaller, everything about me is bigger and bigger and the sounds, louder.

Cannot wait here. I have become very small now. They cannot see me.

You should write a blog. About the discovery – that Jane Austen's Knightley is better than Darcy. That Emma is better than Pride and Prejudice.

And I will run. Like the hunted. I will run…

Don't run. Creep along the walls. Get to the staircase. Get there. Now.

Luxury shops. I don't have the balls to ask the price of those things. Have a Montblanc, though. Got it at a closing. Indian promoters can be so kind when they want to. When you help them make a lot of money. Never used it. What a waste. Kept it for signing major documents but I don't sign any major documents. I am mediocre. I make mediocre documents for others to sign on. Yes. I will write a blog. Self-publish.

Are those bullets…flying past me? Into the walls?

they don't see me running across the few feet to that door have to get in.
DHAG-DHAG-DHAG-DHAG-DHAG
if I move, they will get me.
if I don't move the bullets will wear down the wood to finish me
DHAG-DHAG-DHAG-DHAG-DHAG!

Snap out of it. This is not your dream. There is no door. There is no feeble wood shelter. I don't have to get in. I have to get OUT.

But do you? Wait! Why are we running away from this? We should run towards it, shouldn't we? Someone else will take care of it for us.

It is like jumping in front of a moving train. Do it! Lie down. Rest. Wait for your destiny to consume you. This could be it. Don't run!

Without a letter for them? What about goodbye? What about closure? Like this? Not like this. Not like this. My life. I decide. I do. I will not submit to this. Not like this…

My phone's ringing. Cannot answer. Not now!

Silence it. They shouldn't hear it. They will find you.

I cannot...find it. They cannot hear it. Above the noise that they are making.

Do you not hear the screams?

Oh God! Please help me…

I have to get out. Think. Think. Think.

This is the corridor that goes to the pool. The old lobby. There is a door there. There was a door there. Near the staircase. Yes! I have used it once, to get in.

Was? Did you say there was a door there?

I am not sure…there used to be this entrance that no one seemed to use. We used it once. Just once. I cannot remember…

Can you not get to the pool and out of there?

That was the old entrance to the Taj. Legend has it that it was built the other way around. And that is why what is architecturally the 'back' of the hotel is now its front.

Screw the legend. Is there a way past the pool?

No. there is no way out past the pool. I don't know! Okay? There was a door, which I have used once, near the wood staircase…

Wait! Are you still seeing the wood door from your dream?
Have you not snapped out of it?

DHAG-DHAG-DHAG-TAT-DAT-DHAG-DHAG!
they don't see me running across the few feet to that door.
gunfire still targeted at the vertex shelter...
cannot see me! cannot see me!

This is the dream. I have not snapped out of it.

DHAG-DHAG-DHAG-DHAG-DHAG!

I fly away when no one is looking.

but soon, it will become known...my secret...
I flutter near the high ceiling...
They cannot catch me

But they can shoot me
They are shooting me...the gunmen

green grass. there is grass, hills and trees. blue skies...
telecom towers and skyscrapers...I can fly when I need
to.

The noise is killing me. I want to stop. I want to lie down.
I want to give up. I don't want to be shot in the back. *Not*
like this...

AHHHH!

Don't scream! They will...

They got me. They got me. This is not my dream. And it hurts. It's not like jumping into cold water. It burns. It hurts. Like hell.

I should lie down. Play dead. Be dead. Now. Lie down. Don't crawl. Please don't crawl. The bastards. Don't let them make you crawl...*Your Paradise is Here*...

Deafening. Noise. And smoke. Now there is smoke. The smell of fire. This is it. The smell of gunfire. I remember smells. I remember the smell of horses and stables...and garbage, and dry fish...of Coco, when she was a puppy and Zorro...my sweet, sweet, Zorro. They look at me from the sky. Zorro will wait for me at whatever sort of gate there is...till I get home...and when she sees me...she will admonish me with loud meowing because she is hungry...

I am flying...I see everything...and it is so small...so irrelevant...miniscule...it does not matter...nothing matters.

*   *   *

Glass doors. Yes. Glass doors. Framed with brass. A window...to the world outside. I am flying out of them...I can fly. Road outside. Nearly there. Crawl towards the exit.

My arm. Cannot be sure. The shoulder? The heart? So weak. Can't breathe. Need a rest. So tired.

Get out. They are moving closer. The gunmen…not from the dream…walking towards us…

They cannot see you. They are not shooting at you…

Why is it so calm here? Am I going mad? Is this how it is supposed to be?

I have to get out! In spite of the wound, I can fly…

*   *   *

Out. Now. Shall I lie down?

What *was* that? A gang fight? At the *Taj*?

Why did they shoot me?

Were they shooting me?

Terrorists?

Am I safe? Walk fast. Get to a hospital. Stay there. Will I die in the end?

Lie down. Someone will pick you up.

Don't run. Walk fast. No accidents. Walk fast. Don't run. No accidents, remember? No accidents. The blood. Don't look at it. The blood. Don't look at it. The hellish burning. The hurt. The pain. The baby? The baby? She is not hurt, is she? Please. Please. Please. Please. Wake up. Fetus. Are you there? Did you hear that?

Get to a hospital.

Phone! Did I drop it? Lose it?

Fumble.

Got it. Debbie.

Still calling. This is how a person with one hand lives. This is the physics of the missing limb. I am doing fine. I can do this, no?

"Hi. Where are you? I am near the Taj, okay? Yes. I know about it. This city is mad. You can't come here. There are gunshots and explosions. I am not running, you idiot! Fuck the gasping, Debbie. I will gasp as much as I bloody like. Debbie! SHUT UP! Please! Listen, listen…get to the Naval hospital. Get there. I need an ambulance but don't know how to call for one. Do you? Yes. For me…I am hurt. Badly. I need help. NO! Not your cab…shut up! Get there. Tell them. I need help. I am registered there. I think they will help. Please. Now. Now. Outside the Taj. Headed towards Radio Club. Pavement across the esplanade."

Bhabi! Bhabi! Sister! Oh! Sister!

Calling me? Cab driver. Jesus! Is it the guy who I tricked this morning? He has found me! Holy Cow! Has he found me?

No. No. No. No. No. Not him. That guy had a moustache.

Stopped the cab. I need to lie down. I am going to just sit here now. On the cobbled footpath. Nice and clean. No shit around here. Not even dog poo. Just pigeon droppings. Pigeons are vermin. Just sit down. For a minute. Stopped the cab on the middle of the road. Idiot. What is he shouting for? Leave me alone, Asshole. I need to lie down. On my side. Like this.

He wants to give us a ride. Okay. Lift us up, will ya? I say it like this cool drunken old man in a Western. I can fly. But I will not. No one should know.

"Jaldi nikalna hai, Madam. Bomb phata hai. Police nahin karsakti kuch bhi. Poora Mumbai main chal raha hai. Hospital chalo. Cuffe Parade ki taxi hai."

I want to correct him. No bomb blast, you fool. Machine guns…I think. Deafening gunfire. He's right. What can the police do? Wants to take me to a hospital. Like Dennis Quaid. He wants to rescue us. *Savior*. Crap movie that will play in my head forever. Yes. Same direction. Colaba though, on a parallel road to your destination, cabbie. Naval Hospital. Safe place. The Armed Forces. I love the armed forces.

Frank Hardy in uniform. How sexy is that.

He holds his hand up to the traffic. Making me cross the road. Pushing us into the cab. Damp, stinky interiors. As usual.

He wants us to hold on. Tight. He is going to drive fast. Says he got calls from across the city. We are under attack. Bomb blasts and gunfire. Okay. Can I sit up? Can't lie down in shitty stinky cab, man! Please let me sit up. My arm is not moving. Frozen. No. Not frozen. It has never felt so alive. As it does now. I like the pain. Ignore the pain. Karate class. Rules. Ignore the pain. Don't ever congratulate yourself.

So, it was not a dream.

Why do you keep saying that? Which part of what happened did you not get? This is not a dream! None of it was.

My hands are clammy.
My body is shaking. I have had this feeling before…

the dentist leaps on to my chair like he was mounting a horse
my mouth is open, I make place for his knee on the arm of the chair…
and clutch at whatever I can find on the sides of my helpless body
he beats, struggles, shoves and pushes breathing heavily through his mask

I close my eyes
I hear the creak-cracking of bone and enamel
the full pressure of his body concentrated on my lone tooth
Till suddenly, he pulls out and away…
We are all calm and dignified again
Cotton roll in my mouth, I accept my tooth in a box from him
I keep up the poise but I tremble…they don't notice
But I shake all over…like this…

A deep shaking…not a tremble. A quake that carries you…

Hold onto the filthy seat in front. Hold on.

He is calm. Not driving like a maniac. How is he so calm? Why did he stop for us? Offer me a ride?

Us. He offered us a ride.

Not us. Me. He cannot see you.

He cannot see you.

He cannot see *us*, okay? He sees me. Just me. He called me *sister-in-law*. Then he called me *sister*, when I did not hear him. Then called me madam. *Sister-in-law*. First. Not sister. Because of the baby.

Yes.

The baby.

Why did it take me all these years to figure? I know now for sure. I do not like Mr. Darcy as much as I thought I did.

Mr. Darcy is good, yes. But not good enough. It was always Knightley. Unassuming. Older. Considerate. Consistent. Constant. Maybe a little too strict and perfect but then Emma is exasperatingly juvenile and needs that sort of man. This is one of the greatest discoveries I ever made. I will write about it. It was always Jane Austen's *Emma* and not *Pride & Prejudice* that I liked best.

Ask me again…which is my favourite book? Who is my favourite author? It is Austen and it is *Emma*. *Emma* and Jane Austen. Like coming home. And yes, I wish that I had written it. Written them all, actually. I am going to discuss this with Debbie tonight.
We can discuss it now…

I am not sure we can discuss anything. You already know, don't you? Why would we speak, if you knew what I was going to say? The whole conversation thing, it makes no sense at all. Why would I speak with me when I do in any case speak with me?

You know what? You are a coward and a complete fraud. You ran away. You were bored, you said. By the ordinariness and the mediocrity of your existence and that was a good reason to go. Your mediocrity, which you claim is so great that you'd rather not exist…don't you remember? And here you had the opportunity to let someone finish it for you. No cobblestones, no logistics around organizing a drowning. It would have been like jumping in front of a moving train. You ran. And you got shot. And you ran. You still ran!

Yes! Yes, I did. Egged on by you, or was that me? I don't care. Not like this. I decide. Me. Not anyone else. And we had agreed on drowning.

So you will stick with the plan, then? Complete what we started? Or will this be another of your projects...? Incomplete.

Not your business.

Are you pushing me away? Do you want to talk about it?

No. No! I started the day happy to be alone. I want to be alone.

You cannot let go. You need me. You will never let me go. Can't you see that we are the same? You want me here.

She holds her head and starts to rock back and forth and back and forth.

Tears. She is crying.

At last.

She screams out aloud, "Let me be!"

"It is alright, madam. I will get you to the hospital, okay? I know the place. We are almost there. You will both be alright," says the taxi driver glancing at her in the rear view mirror.

He is so calm. She looks around. Confused. Crying. Alone.

She knows that the driver does not expect her to say anything.
Can she tell him how grateful she is?

– how do you put it in words? Words are like money, they don't mean anything. He stopped for me when he should have been trying to get away, as fast as he possibly could. He saw me...us...

He saw *a face among a million faces, just another woman with no name*...and he stopped. Don't you just love this city? Imagine this happening in Delhi...ha! The cabs there would probably run you over in their hurry to get out. No. It's this city. Brings out the best in you....

The city lights could be an impressionist painting, dancing, streaming and blurring as I pass them by staring, out of the taxi through my tears.

I rock back and forth in a crying trance.

And I enjoy doing that. It's calming. I am ignoring the pain. I will not congratulate myself. Karate. Rules.

Such a flood of tears. The dam is breached. My neck is drenched.

Why are you crying?

Because I died.

In another life…I died just now.

You believe in wonders…something good in everything you see…ABBA, ABBA of your childhood…

We are there. He says. They open the gates after glancing in. There she is, Debbie. Debbie! She is a blur. Tell her to behave. Why the fuck is she screaming?

I have a dream
A fantasy
That helps me through
Reality…

Or was it *helps me cope with reality?* Not sure. Yes I hear ABBA singing it in my head…

Shut up, Debbie! Shut up!

Here's my phone. Call them. Tell them. I am alright. We are alright. Aren't we? Okay?
Just call them? Gosh! Cut the drama, woman.

Think about things that make you happy.

I am at this café…let's call it Delirium
It is dark
I hold my Spanish or Hawaiian or whatever non-electric guitar
The mood is somber
I sing lustily…in ABBA's voice…

…And my destination makes it worth the while
Pushing through the darkness…another mile
I believe in angels…

I sing it with the same high note that ABBA uses and there is this momentary silence

…When I know the time is right for me
I'll cross the stream, I have a dream…

God! The tears. The tears.
We are all singing together…I am at the centre of it all
And I just cannot stop crying…everyone is crying

We have a dream…!
The chorus sounds like a carnival

I like the nurse. She is not freaking out. She asked Debbie to shut up. Good. I like her. All this fuss. A stretcher. Good. I'm home. Don't congratulate yourself. First rule in Karate. I think.

When pleasant thoughts bring sad thoughts to the mind…

Is the converse true? –

She smiles through the tears.

here is a proposition, I say to our friends gathered together
in our new house
The mood is jovial and I am a little bit tipsy
I hold my tonic and gin
I am making love to my tonic and gin, thank you, Billy Joel!
Thank you!
How they laugh…I love entertaining. I'm good. I'm good.
So, as I was saying, if Wordsworth (it was never Longfellow!
Always, Wordsworth!)…so if Wordsworth felt a sweet mood
coming on when pleasant thoughts brought sad thoughts to
the mind, I postulate that the converse is also true…
And ladies and gentlemen, I sit reclined in that very grove
where sat Wordsworth…
And I sink deeper into the wrought iron bench that
we will have on the terrace of the new place…

How they giggle to see me play the jester…
I sit reclined and feel a bitter mood taking over my senses…
when sad thoughts bring happy thoughts to the mind

– yes. Yes. I know. That makes no sense. None of it does.
But I am tipsy on the tonic and gin…drunk out of my
senses…and I can say anything and think anything. You
know what I mean.

then, I feel these eyes on me

Someone who thinks I am very cool...
Who is that?
Staring out at me from behind the sofa
I step out from the centre, leaving the revelry behind...
moving towards that gaze that draws me in

But the sofa keeps moving farther and farther
And the eyes...the eyes...
gleeful, naughty, bright.
Innocent.
The eyes of a child!
I will catch you!

I can fly!
When I want to...when I really, really need to
I start to hover

And I fly over the sofa and behind it...!
we are face to face...

A girl.

Who will she prefer? Darcy over Knightley? Good, and sensitive, and unassuming, and strong. Very strong. Firmness of character. Consistent. Rich. A real man. The ultimate man.

Knightley is the man to love and to worship. The hero. To make an ideal out of. Not Darcy! We liked Darcy because he refused to dance with Lizzy? Why? Look at

Knightley. Consistent. He dances with Harriet…gives consequence to a woman slighted by other men! The obsession, has been so…is so…prejudiced.

Very pretty. Tiny-framed…not broad shouldered like me. She will have a pretty sounding name. Something from Sanskrit…or Hebrew. And sing. And dance. Beautifully.

What is happening to this city? That was no gang war. They were shooting at me. At everyone. They shot that man. Who was running towards me…towards an escape…and it could have been me…lying there. A *victim*. One of many who died before it was time.

… just another woman with no name…
Every day in the morning on her way to the office
You can see her as she catches the train…just a face among a million faces…
Nina, Pretty Ballerina!

But I am not Nina. A woman with no name and no epitaph either…*Your Paradise is Here.*

No it isn't, Peter Kost. We both know that it isn't. My paradise isn't between Dhakuri and Loharkhet either, you know, Peter Kost. That was *your* paradise. And that is because you had no choice…between Dhakuri and Loharkhet…on your way back from the Pindar glacier. White light. Hospital white light. Clean and bright. Green and white walls. Shiny paint. My Paradise, like my destination…*lies a thousand miles.*

That made no sense. Why would Nina, Ballerina sing about a destination? She does not have to walk a thousand miles. It's another song...I am mixing them up. Nina, Pretty Ballerina does not sing *I have a Dream*! Stop mixing them up...

tra la la la laa laa, lies a thousand miles...I remember...! It goes like this,

I have...a dream, a song to sing...to help me cope, with any-thing...

Yes. Those are the lyrics. Finally. I got that right. –

Made in the USA
Columbia, SC
10 May 2024

35111459R00173